MW01127410

THE DUSKHUNTER SAGA

SARA C ROETHLE

Chapter One

An air of foreboding permeated the walls of Castle Helius. Markus and Isolde, when they were around, watched me warily, though I was no threat to either of them. Markus' secret was the same as my own. I wasn't telling anybody.

I had never learned how the Potentate knew I was in danger when he sent the pair to aid me against Karpov. If either of them knew more about it, they weren't sharing.

Or perhaps I was just making everything about me. Maybe the sense of unease just had to do with the looming vampire war. We had told the Potentate what we learned of Karpov's intent, and that others would surely soon pick up his crusade. If the younger vampires managed to kill off the ancients who kept them under control, the Ebon Province would be bathed in blood.

I couldn't let that happen, and not only because the killing of a certain ancient would end my life too.

My boots tapped lightly across the smooth stones leading to the main keep. A messenger had found me that morning with word that the Potentate desired an audience with me. The Seeing Sword rode my shoulder, silent since the night Karpov was killed.

I tossed my red braid behind my back as I opened the heavy oak and iron door. I had acquired new armor since my old set had been lost in Charmant. My leather cuirass forced my back straight, though my shoulders wanted to hunch. I'd been waiting for the moment the Potentate told me he knew everything. That he knew I was a vampire's human servant. The way he'd been watching me in the dining hall told me he at least knew more than he was letting on. He watched me like I was a strange new creature, and he was trying to figure out my use.

I walked past an older hunter as I made my way up the staircase. Surely I was just imagining that he looked at me strangely. I'd heard no whispers behind my back. No one had questioned how such a small band of hunters had managed to kill four ancient vampires along with a slew of young ones. Steifan and Tholdri had been listening closely for such talk, but whenever the event was mentioned it was not with an air of skepticism. Markus, Tholdri, Isolde, and I were highly capable, and Steifan and Niall had told the tale of our bravery. Never mind that none of us would have survived the night if Markus and I weren't both human servants, and if Asher had not been fighting on our side.

I reached the Potentate's door, which swung inward

before I could knock. My eyes landed on the Potentate as I stepped inside.

He stood leaning against his desk, arms crossed. "You appear ready for battle, Lyssandra." The lines around his eyes wrinkled with a small smile. "Do you have a mission I am unaware of?"

I stopped gnawing the inside of my cheek and lifted my chin, moving further into the room. "My only mission is to serve the Helius Order."

His bony shoulders drooped. If I didn't know any better, I'd say he was tired, but men like the Potentate rarely showed weakness.

His intelligent blue eyes glanced me over, eventually settling on the hilt of the Seeing Sword peeking over my shoulder. "How has the Voir L'épée been serving you?"

I shifted my weight to the other foot, feeling uncomfortable standing in the center of the room, but he hadn't invited me to sit. Three chairs sat empty near the cold hearth, and another behind his desk. The wide open door was my only comfort. If we were discussing something important, he would have closed it.

"It is a fine sword," I said. "Finely honed."

He pushed away from his desk, stepping near. Though he had grown thin with age, he was still a head taller than me. His eyes seemed to bore into my skull. "And has it warned you of dangers? Tholdri told me of the Nattmara you slew."

Was he trying to get me to admit that the sword had

spoken to me? It had been his sword, he knew of its gifts, yet he'd never mentioned it.

"It thrums through my mind any time someone means me harm," I said. "If I had realized that's what it did, not just warning me of predators but of any who meant me harm, I might not have come so close to becoming the Nattmara's meal."

His frown let me know I'd misspoke. "I suppose that is my fault for not being clearer?"

My jaw hung open for a moment. "Not at all, it is my fault for misunderstanding. But I learned quickly enough, and it is a fine sword."

He turned away, pacing back toward his desk. I wished he would hurry up and tell me what he wanted with me. I was so nervous it felt like there were sun ants marching up and down my back.

He moved his palm across the worn surface of his desk, keeping his back to me. "You will go to Silgard. A duchess has been found drained of blood. Two of her ladies are missing." He glanced over his shoulder at me. "You will bring Steifan."

"What about Tholdri?"

Suddenly his eyes held a hard glint. "What of him? You may have required aid in defeating Karpov, but this should be a simple task. Slay the monster responsible for killing the duchess, and bring its head to the Archduke. Make sure Steifan learns something this time."

I swallowed my next remark, hiding my blush with a bow. "We will depart at once."

He dismissed me with the wave of a hand.

I counted my steps as I retreated to the door. Mustn't look too eager to escape.

When I was out in the hall, I heaved a sigh of relief, then focused my thoughts on the task ahead. Silgard was the largest city in the Ebon Province. Hunting in such a populous location might prove difficult, especially if the vampire had human servants living within the city walls. The vampire could have any number of well-guarded hiding places.

I walked down the final set of stairs, reaching the main entry, then stepped outside. I needed to gather my belongings, but first I had to find Steifan to ensure he'd be ready to depart. I almost hated to take him into more danger, though he usually fared better than I... which I was sure was just pure dumb luck.

I had only taken a few steps down the stone walkway when a shadow crossed my path. A tall, female shadow. I lifted my eyes, already knowing who it was.

Isolde braced her hands on her hips. She wore a plain cream colored shirt and dark breeches, no armor, so she wasn't going anywhere outside the castle. Her black hair hung in a dark ponytail, leaving her severe features unadorned.

She looked at me as she might a stain on her clean shirt. "What did the Potentate want with you?"

I crossed my arms, jutting my hip out to one side. "And what business is that of yours?"

Her eyes narrowed to mere slits. "You know why—"

I lifted a hand to cut her off. "It's nothing that concerns you or Markus. Simply a mission in Silgard."

Her brows lifted. "In Silgard? And the Potentate is sending *you*?"

I couldn't help my slightly mocking smile. Isolde was my senior, if anyone got to go to Silgard, it honestly should have been her. That thought alone stopped me. Why *had* the Potentate chosen me? Steifan made sense, he would know how to charm the dukes and duchesses, but so would Isolde. Finally, I shrugged in reply, not knowing what else to say.

She didn't seem to notice my sudden worry. With a flick of her ponytail, she gave me a final glare, then turned and walked off.

I glanced at the hilt of the Seeing Sword peeking over my shoulder. "You could've warned me an enemy was nearby," I scoffed, then started walking.

I pushed thoughts of the Potentate and Isolde from my mind. There would be real enemies on the road. And come nightfall, there would probably be vampires. I hoped it wouldn't be anyone I knew.

I SEARCHED THROUGH MY WEAPONS TRUNK, ENSURING I had everything I might need. I already wore my armor and my sword, and had packed two spare sets of clothing. I hoped the mission would take no more than a week, but there really was no saying. It would take several days to ride to Silgard, and hunting the vampire might take more than one night. If it was killing high-ranking nobles whose deaths would be immediately noticed, it was either extremely intelligent, or extremely stupid. If we killed it in one night it was just stupid, and probably new dead. But if the creature eluded us it was older dead, perhaps even ancient and another proponent of Karpov's new order.

I lifted my head at a knock on the door. I'd be leaving soon, so I hadn't locked it. It opened before I could invite the knocker inside. Steifan was the first to enter, followed closely by Tholdri. Steifan was expected, and Tholdri, well I supposed I expected him too, even though he had no reason to delay our mission.

Watching me still kneeling by my trunk, Tholdri walked across the small room and sat on my cream coverlet. He raked a hand through his impressive golden locks, then aimed his speculative gaze at me.

"Don't look at me like that," I sniffed. "The Potentate gave me a mission, and it has nothing to do with Asher."

Tholdri lifted a brow. "How did you know that's what I was thinking?"

Steifan leaned against the wall near the closed door, watching us.

Clutching two spare daggers and a bundle of crossbow bolts, I stood. "Because you've asked me about him every single time I've left the castle."

He shrugged, giving me a charming smile that would

melt lesser women in their boots. "You can't blame me for worrying, Lyss."

I set the weapons on my bed beside him. "I most certainly can. Now is there anything else? I want to put good distance between us and the castle before dark."

"Eager to be away from the Potentate's watchful eye?" he asked.

I shook my head, though in truth that was part of it. "The duchess cannot be given her rites until we examine her. It's warm enough in the South that she will be growing riper by the day. I would not delay our arrival."

I walked across the room to my stuffed saddlebags, wondering how I would fit any more weapons within.

I could feel Tholdri's eyes on my back. "Don't you think it's odd that the Potentate is sending you away so quickly after we told him of the vampire war? You would think he would want one of his best hunters close at hand."

"He has you, and Markus and Isolde. *Someone* has to go to Silgard."

He stood and moved in front of me, preventing me from avoiding his gaze. "And if you see Asher along the way?"

I did better than meeting his gaze, I affixed him with an icy glare. "Then I ignore him. Unless he has news on the vampire situation, I have no use of him."

"I'll be with her," Steifan said from behind my back.

Tholdri and I both looked at him, but Tholdri beat me to saying what we'd both been thinking. "And what difference does that make? She's going to do as she wishes regardless."

Steifan shrugged. "Whatever you say. I just meant I could be there as a voice of reason."

I glared. "I do not need a voice of reason."

"Yes you do," Tholdri and Steifan said in unison.

I sighed and shook my head. "I won't do anything stupid, and I'm anxious to take to the road." I looked to Tholdri. "And I'm just as anxious as you to discover why the Potentate is sending me."

Dismissing Tholdri with a final meaningful look, I turned to Steifan. "Go ready the horses. I'll meet you at the gate shortly." I looked him up and down. He wore his armor and his sword, but . . . "You do have everything you need ready, don't you? I'd hate to delay further."

His eyes darted, giving away his sudden worry. "I'll meet you at the gates shortly. I have only a few more things to attend."

Tholdri walked toward the door and clapped Steifan on the shoulder. "I'll have the stablehand ready your horses."

Steifan's hazel eyes shimmered with relief. "You have my thanks." He opened the door and hurried outside before I could make comment, shutting it quietly behind him.

"Am I really that scary?" I asked Tholdri.

"He doesn't want to disappoint you. I think it's quite sweet." He went for the door, then turned with his hand on the knob. "Promise me you won't do anything stupid, Lyss."

"I've already decided I can't kill Asher when a vampire war is about to begin," I explained. "The order needs me."

He opened the door. "I'll see you soon then, and don't get Steifan killed."

Whatever clever retort I might have thought up was cut off by him exiting and shutting the door behind him. I stared at the door for a minute, then went back to my preparations, sparing the occasional glance for my bookshelf. In a secret cubby behind it was all of my research done to find Asher. So much time wasted, when all I had to do was nearly die to draw him out.

Now I had him, but I wasn't quite sure what to do with him. Part of me still wanted to kill him, to end my existence as a vampire's human servant. But another part of me, a dark hidden part I would never admit to, wasn't sure if I could.

I ARRIVED AT THE GATES BEFORE STEIFAN, AND couldn't quite contain my irritation. The stablehand—a young male hunter whose name I didn't know—quickly handed me my reins with eyes averted. Maybe I *was* scary, or maybe my nerves painted everything in a dark light. Perhaps the stablehand was just distracted and not frightened of me at all.

I stood outside the wooden wall of the stable with my horse and waited. I'd been given a well-muscled brown mare which I'd ridden many times before. While the horses were not assigned to individual hunters, most of us had our preferences, and the young stablehands tended to remember. For eventually, if they trained well, they would climb up the ranks. And any young hunter would do well to be liked by whatever mentor was assigned to them. Anything less might get them killed.

Steifan had never had to remember horses to earn favor. Because of his wealthy family, he'd skipped many steps.

I petted my mare's forehead as the sun shifted high enough in the sky to project our shadows across the dirt road leading toward the gates. Steifan had wasted so much time we wouldn't make it far before dark. Normally I would travel through the night, but that might not be wise given the state of things. If vampires wanted to kill freely, they'd be keen to eliminate vulnerable hunters.

I watched as another shadow was added to mine and the horse's, but didn't react.

"Isolde told me of your mission," Markus' voice said to my back.

I shifted my stance, bringing him into sight. "Yes? What of it?"

He pushed a short lock of brown hair away from his strong-jawed face. He wore a simple white shirt with pearl buttons, and tan woolen breeches, no armor. So like

Isolde, he was not on assignment and could have been sent to Silgard instead of me. "I just think it's odd that you're being sent so far away under the circumstances. If it is a simple killing, one of the lesser ranking hunters could have been sent."

I sucked my teeth. "Yes, it has been established that it is quite odd, but I'm not sure what anyone expects me to do about that. The Potentate orders and I obey." My horse tugged at its reins, upset that I'd turned my attention away without offering any treats. I gave her the rein's full length so she could snuffle at the ground, even though there was no grass to be found.

Markus' playful smirk made his face seem a little less harsh. "You follow orders? You could have had me fooled."

I laughed, relaxing. I wasn't used to having any sort of repartee with Markus, but he was at least slightly less sour toward me than Isolde. Perhaps it was because we shared the same secret, though we had discussed it no further since I first learned he was also a vampire's human servant.

I scanned the road to the courtyard beyond for any sign of Steifan, then turned back to Markus. "I obey where it matters, and I have an inkling you do the same."

"Yes we are similar in that way, I suppose," he agreed. He spotted Steifan at the same time I did, carrying two heavy saddlebags brimming with who knew what. "This is goodbye then. Do take care you return to us."

I looked to see if he was being sarcastic, but he had

already turned to walk away, and Steifan was nearly upon me. His black chin-length hair fell forward over his reddened face, flushed either with the effort of hauling the heavy bags, or out of embarrassment.

The stablehand spotted him and approached with a second horse, a white and gray dappled mare.

I nodded a greeting to Steifan as he reached my side, then looked up at the sky. The sun had moved again. We'd be lucky to make it to a village before dark. While Bordtham and Charmant could both be reached in a day's ride to the north, villages were more spread out to the south and east until you got closer to Silgard.

Once Steifan's saddlebags were strapped to his horse, he turned to me. "It really wasn't my fault. My father happened to arrive just as I was getting ready to depart. Now I have an entire list of nobles I am supposed to endear myself to in Silgard, including Duke Auclair, the victim's husband."

I pursed my lips. "Well I don't envy you that, but let us first focus on making it to a village before nightfall. I have an eerie feeling in my bones, and I'd rather not rest without a locked door between us and vampires."

The stablehand glanced between us with wide eyes, then scurried away.

Steifan watched him go. "You do have a habit of scaring people, don't you?"

I scowled. "Hurry up and mount, or I'll be forced to scare you too."

Steifan did as he was asked while I climbed into my

own saddle, then angled my horse toward the nearby gates, which were already opening for us. A few hunters stopped to watch us depart, and I startled, recognizing a face well behind them near the door to the main keep.

The Potentate stood alone, tall and wiry, but still strong. He watched me go, that same strange expression on his face, like I was a creature entirely new to him. He'd never watched me like that previously, only since I had returned with news of Karpov's death.

I wasn't sure what had changed, and it was debatable whether I really wanted to know. I knew better than most that some secrets were best left buried.

Chapter Two

We reached Silgard on the evening of the third day after leaving Castle Helius. We'd made camp near villages too small to have inns the first two nights, and stayed at an inn the third night closer to the city. There had been no vampires, nor Nattmara, nor anything else. I almost felt foolish for being so worried, but I knew all too well that being bold would get you killed. When you're a hunter worry is a virtue, even when unwarranted.

Steifan and I were both deep in our own thoughts as our horses plodded down the wide dirt road leading up to the city built atop a hill. We passed farms and peasant dwellings, the chimneys leaking smoke to flavor the air. It was a nicer thing to notice than the underlying scent of manure tightening my throat. My sharp senses were a blessing at times, but could also prove a curse.

As we started up the incline, farms shifted to more

homes, and a few merchants with carts. My stomach growled as we passed a cart with honey rolls, but we could not in good conscience delay any further. The duchess' body was probably smelling far worse than the manure.

"What do we do once we reach the city?" Steifan asked.

I gazed at the distant metropolis, its walls twice as high as those of Castle Helius and made from pale gray stone. "We seek out Duke Auclair. We'll need to observe the duchess so she can be given her rites. If we are lucky, the duke will offer us a meal and a place to stay, as is customary, but I have not come to expect it. Few want a red-haired *witch* within their estate."

He straightened in his saddle and blinked at me. "Truly, you were not offered lodgings on those grounds?"

I shrugged. "Old tales tend to linger." In truth I could have changed my hair color, there were many ways to stain or lighten one's hair, but I'd never tried. I knew the color had to have been passed down by one of my ancestors, and with so few of my relations still living, I clung to that small connection.

Steifan turned his attention to the city gates as we approached. The portcullis stood open with just two city guards posted to question visitors. It didn't seem a good way to protect the city to me, but then again, Silgard, the Capital of the Ebon Province, had not suffered siege in over a century. Between the Capital and the other provinces lay the mires, desolate forests, vampires, and ghouls. Further south was the Merriden Sea, an impassible expanse. If the vampires weren't enough to scare away conquerors, the lack of motivation to acquire such cursed lands would do the trick. Though Silgard was as large as any great city, the rest of the province left much to be desired.

We dismounted as we reached the wide bridge leading to the gates, and I wondered how many vampires were lurking within the walls. Other provinces had them too, but none could rival the Ebon Province in number of undead. Maybe it was the lack of sunlight that drew them, or perhaps many of the lines simply originated in my homeland and never branched out.

The guards standing to one side of the entryway were both older men wearing polished breastplates over midnight blue livery. They looked at our hardened leather armor skeptically as we approached, as if unaware Steifan and I could probably throw them into the open canal below with little effort.

"We weren't told to expect the Helius Order," one said.

I furrowed my brow, holding my mare's reins taught to keep her close behind me. "Were you not informed of Duchess Auclair's murder?"

They locked gazes for a moment, then the one who'd spoken shrugged. "Many believe the murder wasn't actually committed by a vampire. I did not think the Order had been contacted."

"We were told there was no question to the murder,"

Steifan cut in. "What do you mean it wasn't committed by a vampire?"

Another knowing glance between the guards. "Forget we said anything," the more vocal guard continued. "The duke's estate is on the northern end of the city, further up the hill. Head that way then ask around, most anyone will be able to point you in the right direction. Duke Auclair is a well-known man."

They both turned their attention forward, making it clear we were dismissed.

I shrugged to Steifan, then led my horse into the city. The wide stones of the bridge turned to cobbles, spreading before us to form a central court. Merchants gathered here, backed by stables and an inn on one side, and short wooden homes on the other. Beyond the inn I could see the tall arched roof of the guild hall.

The chatter of voices as we walked further into the square was both comforting and unnerving. I couldn't pick out any specific conversations, but surely some were remarking on our arrival. I supposed I would never know what was said, but it was still nice being in a city outside Castle Helius.

I received curious glances from market goers on all sides as I led the way toward the stables. I was sure there would be separate stables near the duke's estate, but after the strange words of the guards I wasn't keen on leaving my horse there.

We didn't make it far before a courier in green and gold livery stopped us. He was young, probably only twelve or thirteen, with sandy hair and freckles that made him look even younger.

He shifted his eyes between me and Steifan, finally settling firmly on Steifan. "Duke Auclair tasked me with waiting here every day for your arrival. He'll be pleased to see you shortly. You can stable your horses within the White Quarter."

I appreciated Steifan looking to me for instruction.

I clutched my reins protectively. "We will stable our horses here, then you will lead us to the duke's estate."

The courier opened his mouth like he wanted to argue, then his eyes flicked to the sword visible over my shoulder and his mouth snapped shut. He bowed his head. "As you wish. The White Quarter is not far."

I had already deduced as much. In the distance a cobbled path led upward from the square, lined with a secondary inner wall. Tall roofs towered beyond that wall, their white shingles glaring in the sun. I was betting the duke lived somewhere behind those walls. Curious, that the vampire would risk the well-guarded area instead of preying on the peasants outside the city walls. Maybe the guards were right and it wasn't a vampire. Either way, the murder was probably personal. Not a random killing. If the only need was blood or death, a duchess was not necessary.

The courier and Steifan were both watching me, and I realized I'd gotten lost in my thoughts.

I cleared my throat, then tugged my mare's reins, continuing toward the stables. The courier was given the choice of either moving out of my way, or getting trampled by my horse. He moved.

We stabled our horses, then rented a room at the inn to store our belongings. Once we were ready, we followed the courier toward the duke's estate. I noticed the market goers sparing more glances for the courier than they did for Steifan and me. His livery made it clear to which noble he belonged. Just what type of duke was this man who made city guards nervous, and whose courier drew more curiosity than a red-haired hunter?

I could feel eyes on my back as we started up the cobblestone expanse toward the wealthy estates. The path wound upward, bordering the tall wall guarding the homes to our left. To the right of the path were shops and more modest wooden homes.

Eventually we reached wrought iron gates and two more city guards, this pair younger and more alert than those outside the main wall.

Both guards wordlessly observed the courier, then looked us up and down. "You'll need to leave your swords," one said.

Standing straight I was taller than one guard and Steifan was taller than both, but I didn't think these two men would be intimidated by size. Regardless, they were fools if they thought they would part me from my sword.

"We are here to hunt a vampire," I said. "We will not be without our swords."

"It's daylight," one guard said tiredly.

He did have a point, but I still wasn't giving up my

sword. I was tired from our travels, and ready for a hot meal and a pint of ale. As I saw it, these two guards were the only thing standing between me and that end.

"Lyss—" Steifan began, likely noting the change in my expression.

But I was already stepping forward past the courier toward the guard. "Look, you can try and physically take my sword from me, which I do not recommend, or you can explain to Duke Auclair why his wife will spend another day rotting in her bedroom waiting for us to avenge her murder."

The guard to my right audibly swallowed, the one I was eyeing paled.

The pale one gave a curt nod. "I suppose if I escort you, and the duke accepts your presence with weapons, then we can allow you to pass."

I wanted to say, *There, was that so hard?* But I knew better than to press my luck. I accepted his offer with a nod. "Lead the way."

I stepped back as the guard who would remain behind opened the ornate gate, letting the rest of us pass through before shutting it behind us. The other led the way past a grouping of stables, down a wide expanse between estates. He walked with stiff shoulders, nose lifted.

As we walked Steifan gave me a look that told me I should behave.

I wrinkled my nose, but nodded. He was likely worried that word of my rude actions would make it back to his father. I felt sympathy for his position, but *he* was the one here to charm nobles. I was just here to solve a murder.

More confident now that he was within the secondary walls, the courier scurried forward to lead the way while the guard seemed to think better of keeping his back to us and fell into step beside Steifan.

I smiled to myself. The guard had deemed Steifan the greater threat, the one who needed to be watched more closely. *Amateur.*

My grin faded as I caught a glimpse of an oddly familiar face beyond the wrought iron fence of one estate's expansive garden. I blinked, and the face was gone. Had I just imagined it? I didn't have time to consider it further as the courier stopped before the tall wooden door of a particularly grand estate.

We waited at the base of three wide stone steps leading up to the door while the courier knocked. Almost immediately the door swung inward, revealing a servant in the duke's livery, an older man who seemed relieved to see us.

He gave the guard a quick, questioning glance, but waved us in, stepping back and holding the door wide.

Steifan and I stepped inside and glanced around. The floor beneath our boots was pristine marble, matching white walls rising tall overhead. Bookshelves lined the sitting room, though they held few books and even fewer trinkets. While the home was grand, the decor was oddly sparse. The smell of a rotting corpse hung in the air.

A man came down the adjoining stairs to greet us, presumably the duke. He looked us over with small eyes set in a ruddy face. At our backs, the servant who'd opened the door was arguing with the guard on whether or not he would be allowed inside.

The duke straightened his stiff crimson lapels, ignoring the arguing men in favor of regarding us. "You are late. It's preposterous how long I have been asked to hold my wife's body. She deserves her rites." With jerky movements, he swept his hand over his thinning silver hair, fluttering it down to flatten his well-oiled beard.

Steifan swooped into a ridiculous bow. "My apologies, Duke Auclair. We have ridden many nights from Castle Helius to reach you. I am Steifan Syvise, son to Gregor Syvise. My father sends his greetings, and his condolences."

I snapped my jaw shut. I knew Steifan was practically nobility, but I'd never seen him act the part. His words seemed to placate the duke.

We turned at the sound of commotion as the guard pushed past the door servant, charging inside. The courier followed, reaching out helplessly to stop him. The servant stood stiff-spined near his post.

"Duke Auclair." The guard bowed his head, then quickly raised it. "The hunters would not relinquish their weapons. I wanted to ensure they were welcome in your presence."

The duke's face grew ruddier. "They are hunters, you fool!" He waved his hands. "What good are they to us without their weapons? They must find the creature who killed my wife."

At this point I would've interjected to calm the flustered men, but I was too busy trying not to breathe in the scent of rotting corpse coming from upstairs. Could the men not smell it? It was only comfortably warm outside, but I had a feeling the upper rooms must amplify the heat to produce such a smell.

The guard and courier were muttering apologies while the servant watched the duke to see how he would react. Steifan seemed unsure if it was his place to intervene. What I wouldn't give to be hunting in a small village away from such ridiculous men.

The duke's body grew stiff as the guard continued to convince him that he had done the right thing in escorting us. "Silence!" The duke snapped. "Everyone away except the hunters. Make sure we are not disturbed."

I'd never seen two men and a boy move so fast. In mere moments Steifan and I were alone with the duke.

"This way," the Duke said blandly, gesturing up the stairs.

It made me wary that his anger could disappear so quickly. I wondered what other emotions lurked just below the surface. But that was a worry for later. I led the way up the stairs, overly conscious of the sound of my boots on the painted wood. The rest of the house was utterly silent.

I reached the top and stepped aside to wait for the

duke, pretending I didn't know which direction to go in. Steifan came up last, and I fell into step beside him as the duke led us down a wide hall adorned with the longest rug I'd ever seen. Following the putrid smell, my eyes landed on the door before the duke stepped in front of it. It wasn't as hot up here as I imagined. It should have taken the body longer to stink.

"I'd rather not see her like this," the duke said as he opened the door. "I'll wait out here."

I nodded, then stepped inside the room. As soon as I was out of the duke's line of sight, I lifted my sleeve to cover my nose and mouth.

Steifan moved to my side, already looking green. Together, we looked down at the bed.

The duchess wore nothing but a night shift, the fabric sheer enough to clearly show her wilted shape beneath. She had probably been stripped when the corpse was examined. Graying ringlets were plastered back from her snow white face. As reported, there were two small puncture wounds in the side of her neck, but that wasn't what held my interest. The way her curls dried made it seem like they'd been sopping wet when she'd been laid up on the bed. Parts of her shift were stained brownish yellow, like blood had been washed away. I wanted to speak my observations out loud to Steifan, but had little doubt the duke would be listening from outside the door. I didn't want him to hear me, because no one had mentioned the body being tampered with. I'd guess she was moved long after her death. It explained the lack of blood on the wound, and the water stains. Just how long had the duchess been missing before her death was finally reported?

I leaned closer, my nose and mouth still covered by my sleeve, for what good it did against the stench. Judging by her skin, I didn't think the rotting had occurred while she'd been submerged in water, more like she died, rotted, then had gotten wet far after the fact.

I straightened, giving the rest of the room a quick glance. Nothing stood out—other than Steifan looking close to retching in the corner. The dresser was tidy with only a few visible trinkets, just like in the sitting room. I would have liked to peruse the drawers, but had a feeling the duke would intervene. I didn't want to let him know I suspected anything. Not just yet.

I motioned for Steifan to exit the room ahead of me. The duke still waited for us in the hall.

I searched his expression, looking for hints of guilt. If the guards at the main gate didn't think she was killed by a vampire, did they perhaps suspect her husband? Either way, something was very wrong here. "I was informed she was found in her bed, deceased," I said simply.

The duke puffed up his cheeks. "That is correct, this is where I found her. Her body was damp, but I do not know why."

I cleared my throat, trying to rid myself of the clinging smell of death. Perhaps he was telling the truth. Maybe someone else put her there. "Do you have any enemies? Anyone who would do this to your wife to horrify you?"

Sweat shone on his brow as he shook his head. "Wealth breeds enemies, but I can think of no one in particular."

I sighed. He was definitely hiding something, but what, was yet to be determined. "I'll need a list of all of her friends," I explained, "and any places she frequented. If she kept a journal, seeing that would be helpful."

The duke's tiny eyes went so wide they bulged. "Questioning her friends, I understand, but what use would you have for her journal? Is she not deserving of her privacy?"

Steifan stepped closer. "Often vampires will stalk their prey for days or weeks before attacking. Sometimes journals can reveal if the victim noticed anyone watching them, or if they recently met someone new. It might even provide a physical description."

I gave him an approving look. He was learning.

The duke's already thin lips thinned further, disappearing into his beard. "Well I," he paused, "I don't know where Charlotte kept her journal. I'll search for it."

I bet you will, I thought. *And once you find it, you'll burn it.* Outwardly, I smiled. "That will be very helpful. In the meantime we'll get started questioning her close friends. When did her two ladies go missing?"

The duke seemed to calm himself. "The first left us weeks before my wife's death, the other shortly after.

Their bodies were never found, so I don't know if the vampire took them, or if they simply fled."

I nodded, taking in his words. "And Charlotte's friends?"

"My courier should be able to provide you with a list. He ran all of Charlotte's errands and scheduled her outings. Now if you don't mind, I'd like to prepare my wife for her rites."

Steifan and I both bowed. Steifan because it was the proper etiquette, and me to hide my calculating expression. There was something wildly off about Charlotte's murder, and her husband's behavior, and I fully intended to find out what that was.

For while my purpose was to hunt vampires, it was also to avenge innocent lives. I wasn't sure what type of monster had caused Charlotte's demise, but I would see that monster brought to justice, even if it was the man standing before me.

Chapter Three

The servant held the door for us as we walked outside, duteously avoiding eye contact. The young courier waited below the three steps leading down to the street. The guard who had escorted us was gone. Apparently he'd done his duty.

I looked down at the courier as the door shut behind us. "You are to give us a list of all of the duchess' friends and places she frequented," I explained. "If you know what her schedule was a few days before she was killed, that would also be helpful."

The courier stepped back, looking to Steifan as if expecting him to dispute my words. When he didn't, the courier nodded quickly, splaying short hair across his forehead. "I can escort you. The duchess had few friends. I can show you where they live."

What was this, I thought, *someone actually being helpful?* "What's your name?" I asked.

His flush hid his freckles. "Bastien Goddard, my lady." He dipped his sandy head in a bow.

I realized then that he didn't keep looking to Steifan because he was male and therefore in charge. I just made him nervous in the way many women make young boys nervous.

I smiled. "Pleasure to meet you, Bastien. We will follow your lead."

Bastien lifted his head and was off like a colt.

Steifan leaned near my shoulder as we hurried after him. "That's the nicest I've ever seen you be to, well, anyone."

"Oh shut up," I said, not wanting to embarrass Bastien.

My grin faded as we followed Bastien into another square, much smaller than the one at the entrance of the city. I'd realized why I found the boy's demeanor charming. He reminded me of Elizabeth, the last person to find me worth interest. She hadn't been frightened spending time with a hunter either, and it had gotten her killed.

Bastien stopped walking at the edge of the square and turned to us. "Lady Montrant lives over there." He pointed past gilded carts bearing pastries, cakes, and meat pies. "But she should be out here soon, most of the noble ladies take tea at this time."

I followed his finger as it moved to point at a gathering of wrought iron tables. Many ladies gathered there, and my first thought was how did they move in all that fabric? And how did their heads remain upright with such tall hair? I'd seen such garb on rare occasions growing up, but I was far more used to village girls in simple dresses, with their hair hanging in practical plaits.

A woman emerged from the home Bastien had pointed out. Her lilac dress looked like it weighed more than three other ladies' dresses put together. Her hair was pure silver with age, but appeared silken in texture, piled into artificial ringlets atop her head. Jewels embellished her bodice and her throat.

"That's her?" I asked Bastien.

"Yes, Lady Montrant. She and the duchess were close friends for many years."

I looked to Steifan. "Find a place with Bastien to look inconspicuous. I want to know if anyone watches me questioning the lady with too much interest. Don't question anyone, just note who might be watching and ask Bastien for their names."

Steifan seemed hesitant. "Do you want to question her yourself? Are you sure you know how to speak properly?"

I scowled. "They will understand my words well enough."

Bastien tugged Steifan's sleeve. "Come, I know just the place. No one will notice us watching."

Steifan gave me one last hesitant look, then allowed Bastien to guide him away.

I turned my attention to Lady Montrant, now seated at a table with two other ladies while a servant poured them tea. I started walking toward them, then froze mid-step, sensing a dull thrum of energy from the Seeing Sword. It was the first time it had awoken since the night of Karpov's death.

I looked around, but no one was watching me, let alone threatening me. Perhaps it was nothing, though it did make me realize the sword had been quiet around the duke. If he was trying to cover up his wife's murder, surely the sword would have seen him as a threat?

I shook my head minutely and kept walking, stopping in front of Lady Montrant's table.

"My ladies," I said, encompassing the two younger women with Lady Montrant in my gaze. "Do you mind if I join you?" I gestured to the empty chair at their table.

The two younger women seemed to shrink as they looked up at me, while Lady Montrant seemed to grow. Her spine stiffened and her narrow nose raised. "I imagine this is about Charlotte? I can see no other reason for a hunter to be in this part of the city."

I ignored the subtle insult, not bothering to argue that many hunters came from noble families, and could fit in well amongst the wealthy. "Yes, this is about Charlotte. I'm told you and she were close friends. I'd like to ask you a few questions."

"Close friends." She snorted. "Very well, have a seat."

I pulled out the remaining seat and lowered myself less than gracefully, snatching one of the pastries from the table on my way down. Lady Montrant already didn't like me, so I might as well skip the niceties.

I took a bite of the pastry, chewed and swallowed. "Were Duke and Duchess Auclair struggling with coin?"

The lady's jaw fell open, showing healthy teeth, a rarity in someone her age. Or at least a rarity in the small villages. I imagined many in this part of the city still had all their teeth. She shut her jaw with a click. "Why would you think such a thing?"

"I was just at their home. It is a grand estate, but there are few grand treasures within." I took another bite of pastry, enjoying the sweet, flaky crust.

The lady seemed to think about her answer while her two companions pretended they were not in the middle of our conversation, politely sipping their tea.

She started to reach for her own tea, then pulled her gloved hand away. "Very well. Yes, Charlotte was struggling with coin. I grew tired of sponsoring her every time we were out. I told her as much roughly two weeks ago. I now feel great remorse for what I said to her."

She didn't look like she felt great remorse. She looked like she didn't really care at all that her friend was gone.

I decided on another tactic. "Do you know if Charlotte felt like anyone was watching her? Had she met anyone new?"

The Lady Montrant smiled a secretive smile, deepening the furrows around her thin lips. "Charlotte met many new people, if you understand my meaning."

Was she implying that Charlotte was less than faithful in her marriage? Perhaps to earn extra coin? I couldn't think of any way to ask my questions that wouldn't have the lady calling for guards to escort me away, but I would remember the implication.

"Do you know if Charlotte kept a journal?" I asked.

The Lady Montrant stood, her movements quickly echoed by the two younger ladies. The lady looked down at me. "If Charlotte had a journal, it would be filled with the blatherings of a simpleton. Now if we're quite finished, I have things to do."

I nodded. "If I have further questions, I'll visit your home."

Her eyes went wide for just a heartbeat, but I didn't miss it, and I would remember it. "Very well," she snapped, then turned and walked away. Her two ladies curtsied, then followed Lady Montrant across the square.

I watched them go, then looked down at the platter of uneaten pastries, and the three mostly full cups of tea. I highly doubted the lady had anywhere urgent to be. She had planned on a long teatime.

I took another pastry for myself, and two more, one for Steifan and one for Bastien. We now had two suspects in the crime, the duke, and the Lady Montrant. I was anxious to see if Steifan and Bastien had spotted any more to add to the list.

I stood and looked around, remembering the slight warning from the Seeing Sword. While a few ladies watched me curiously, none watched threateningly.

But the threat was another thing to remember. Just because I was around *civilized folk*, didn't mean I could lower my guard. If anything, it meant I should raise it.

BASTIEN AND STEIFAN FOUND ME AS I MEANDERED back in the direction of the duke's estate. Bastien's hiding place had indeed been a good one, because I hadn't been able to pick them out from the growing crowd. The three of us walked down a small side street, and I handed each of them a pastry.

Bastien looked at me like I was his new favorite person.

I wiped away my smile, then turned my attention to Steifan. Mustn't get too attached. "Did you notice anyone?"

Steifan tucked a lock of black hair behind his ear, glancing out toward the main street warily. "Everyone was watching you, but most just glanced your way curiously. We did see the servant we met at the duke's estate, but he never looked your way. Perhaps he tried *too* hard to not look your way."

I turned to Bastien, who had devoured his entire pastry in three bites. "What do you know of him? Have you worked with him for long?"

Bastien wiped a fleck of frosting from his lip. "His name is Vannier, I am not sure of his surname. As far as I know, he has always served the duke. He speaks to me little, except to relay my tasks for the day."

I stroked my chin in thought. "Three suspects for our list then. The duke, whose motives are yet unclear. The Lady Montrant, because her former friend borrowed too much coin. And Vannier." I looked down at Bastien. "Was Duchess Auclair a cruel mistress?"

Bastien shrugged. "She was nicer than the duke. She looked down her nose at everyone, but at least she didn't have a temper."

Steifan watched me intently, seeming to absorb every word.

"Questions?" I asked.

"I'm just wondering why you haven't mentioned the vampire. We saw the bite. Do you think it was staged?"

I shook my head. "No, I don't think it was staged, I'm just not sure it's what killed her. Lady Montrant implied that Charlotte spent time with men for coin. I don't think a vampire would be beyond paying for blood if he was trying to remain well hidden within the city. It would explain why he would bite a duchess rather than taking a peasant."

Steifan stared at me wide-eyed. "You mean she *willingly* let a vampire bite her?"

I shrugged. "If she was desperate enough, it's a possibility. Whatever is going on here is dire enough to have resulted in a murder. We cannot afford to ignore any possibilities." I snapped my mouth shut, realizing I probably shouldn't be saying all of this in front of Bastien. He did, after all, work for the duke. He could be a spy.

I observed his intrigued and somewhat excited expression. I really didn't think he was a spy, he seemed to be having too much fun. But you never knew. I needed to be more careful around him.

Steifan looked back toward the main street again as a well-dressed couple passed by. We had all gone silent, so they didn't notice us.

"What now?" Steifan asked once the couple was out of hearing range.

I looked up at the sun. "We still have a few hours until evening. I want to question some of the common folk in the city before dark. Their lips might be a bit looser about things concerning the Duchess and Duke Auclair." I didn't think we'd be hunting any vampires tonight, but we would still search. I wanted to know as much as possible before we went out into the dark.

I turned to Bastien. "This is where we leave you, for now. Do you think you can meet us again tomorrow? I may want to question more of Charlotte's friends."

He grinned and nodded excitedly. "I can wake up early to take care of any tasks the duke might have for me. I could meet you an hour after dawn."

I nodded. "Meet us in the main market square. We'll be waiting."

With that, he hurried off.

"So you really didn't see anyone else watching with interest?" I asked Steifan.

He shook his head. "No one that stood out, though I had an uneasy feeling, like someone was watching me that I couldn't see."

I once again thought of the warning from my sword, and of the face I had glimpsed when we first entered the White Quarter. "Be on your guard, Steifan. I have a feeling we have fallen into something much bigger than the Potentate could have known. We'll stay at the inn near the market tonight. I don't want to be anywhere near the duke's estate while we sleep."

"Agreed," he said as we started walking. "I'll have nightmares enough about Charlotte's corpse tonight."

I smirked. "Stay with me, and you'll eventually collect enough nightmares to last a lifetime."

His black hair lifted in the breeze as he glanced at me. "You know Lyss, I don't doubt that at all."

"Then you're learning," I said more somberly as we headed toward the gate.

And he would continue to learn. Someday he would kill just as easily as I did, and part of me would mourn that day. My life was not something I would wish upon anyone, let alone a friend.

Chapter Four

We learned little more that evening, except that there were more people missing than just the duchess' ladies. It wasn't uncommon for people to go missing in such a large city, but it did seem an unusual amount. We ended up at the inn where we had rented a room upon our arrival to the city. There had only been one room available, which was well enough, as it saved coin. If Steifan was uncomfortable with the impropriety of the situation, well, he'd just have to deal with it.

We had a meal of smoked trout and honeyed ale, then returned to our room. We would rest a short while, then go out into the night to see if I could sense any vampires.

I unlocked the door and entered first, observing the lone bed, wash basin, and our belongings in the corner. My eyes darted back to the bed, realizing there was a yellow daisy there. Steifan pushed into the room behind me and I lunged toward the bed, snatching the flower and crushing it in my palm behind my back. I whipped around as Steifan shut the door.

Steifan narrowed his eyes at me. "Why are you standing like that?"

I relaxed my shoulders, still hiding the crushed daisy. "I just realized I had wanted to check on the horses one last time before we rested. I'll be right back."

His continued gaze said he didn't believe me, but after a moment, he nodded.

When he turned his back to fetch something from the saddlebags, I hurried out of the room, shutting the door quickly behind me. I looked at the crushed flower in my hand, fueling my budding anger, because I knew exactly who it was from. What right had Asher to follow me here? And to know which room I rented? He'd probably bespelled the innkeep into telling him while Steifan and I had been busy with our evening meal.

I hurried down the hall and down the stairs before Steifan could think to follow me. Once I was outside, I dropped the daisy on the ground, then headed for the stables. If Asher was around, he would find me.

I was checking over our horses when I sensed a presence at my back. I turned to find Asher leaning against a thick wooden post supporting the roof of the stable. He stood in profile, his face partially obscured by his long white hair draped over his black coat.

"You should know by now I'm not impressed by dramatic entrances," I chided.

He turned his face toward me and smiled. "Yes, you are impressed by very little." The light from one of the lanterns illuminating the stable hit his face just right, cutting across one silver eye and one high cheekbone.

I crossed my arms and leaned my back against my horse's pen. "Why are you here? We are a long way from the mires."

He pushed away from the post and closed the distance between us. "I wanted to ensure you wouldn't get into any more trouble. You seem to attract it from all directions."

I wanted to back up, but I had effectively trapped myself with the pen behind me. My horse nudged my shoulder, reminding me that it was there. "You didn't come all this way just to keep me out of trouble. Why are you really here?"

"One of the ancients who maintained the old order was killed recently. I had hoped you could help me hunt the culprits. When I searched for you, I could hardly sense you. I didn't expect you to travel so far."

My breath caught at his words. If an ancient had been killed, that meant there were indeed other vampires carrying forth Karpov's plan. I exhaled, then sucked in a sharp breath. "When did it happen?"

"Two nights ago," he explained. "Quite the coincidence that you were sent to a far off city not long before, if my estimations of your travel time are accurate."

I narrowed my eyes. "The Potentate sent me here. There was no way he could have known that one of the ancients was to be killed. I imagine you have ruled out the possibility of the kill being claimed by a hunter?"

He nodded slightly, his gaze intent on my face. "I smelled no humans around the corpse, nor did I recognize the scent of the vampires."

"So what does this mean?" I pressed. "How close are we to a vampire war?"

He arched a white brow. "Dear Lyssandra, we are already at war, just a more subtle war than those waged by mortals."

I wasn't bold enough to think that me being sent away could have anything to do with the ancient's *murder*. Was I actually thinking of the slaying of a vampire as a murder?

I scowled. "So you are at war then, we knew this was coming. Why travel all the way to Silgard to tell me? There's nothing I can do to help you until I solve the murder here. Even once I return to Castle Helius, I may not want to help you."

He splayed one palm against my horse's pen near my shoulder, leaning forward but not quite touching me. He never seemed to touch me unless I was dying and needed to be saved. "For now, we are on the same side. We both want to prevent the slaughter of mortals. So I do believe you will help me, whether you want to or not."

I tucked my arms in tightly against my body to keep from being too close to his hand. "You are insufferable."

"You spoke of a murder here," he continued like I

hadn't spoken. "Perhaps if I help you solve it, you can return to aid me more quickly."

I stiffened. "I don't need your help. You know nothing about being a hunter."

"You are training that other hunter, the one you seem to be sharing a bed with tonight. Surely you can tell me enough that I may be of use."

I ignored the subtle insinuation. If he wanted to think something was going on with Steifan, then so be it. It made no difference. I wanted to tell him to go drown in a swamp, then I realized that he might actually be useful.

"You have thought of something," he said, watching my expression.

"There is something you could do to help, but you will do it only to help solve a murder, because it is the right thing to do. Not as a favor where I will owe you something in return."

He leaned a little closer and lowered his voice, "Name it, and it will be done."

I rolled my eyes to hide my discomfort, ignoring his cool breath on my skin. "I would like to find the murdered woman's journal, but my worry is that if her husband finds it first he will burn it, if he hasn't burned it already. If he has, search her room for anything suspicious."

His brows raised and he leaned back. "You would like me to break into a mortal's home?"

I nodded. "It's one of the large estates up the hill.

You should be able to follow the smell of rotting corpse. I imagine her body will not be burned until tomorrow."

He smiled tightlipped, hiding his fangs. "Very well, I will fetch it shortly. Where will you meet me once the task is done?"

"Steifan and I will be out searching the city for vampires. I imagine you'll be able to find me."

His palm still braced beside me, he leaned forward again. "There are many vampires within the city, Lyssandra. Be careful what you dig up."

"Would a vampire ever pay a mortal woman for blood?" I asked abruptly.

My question seemed to catch him off guard. He took a moment to think about it. "Perhaps, if one was in jeopardy of being discovered, and did not want to flee their territory."

"Have you ever paid for blood?" I regretted the question as soon as I asked it.

The edges of his mouth ticked up. "Dear Lyssandra, I never pay for something I can easily get for free."

With that, he was gone, leaving me alone with my thoughts. I patted my horse's cheek, then left to find Steifan. I didn't know how long it would be until Asher returned with the journal, so I'd just have to drum up *trouble* as quickly as I could.

Chapter Five

A few hours later, Steifan and I walked down the quiet nighttime street. I had relented and told him about my meeting with Asher. Better to explain it while we were alone, rather than explaining it once Asher showed up with the journal. *If* he showed up with the journal. It might already be gone, leaving us no other clues.

"I can't believe he followed you all the way here," Steifan said, breaking the silence as we meandered down an alleyway. I had sensed vampires a few times, but we were yet to come close enough to seek them out.

"He didn't follow me," I snapped. "He only sought me out after the ancient was killed."

"Yes, because a young huntress will surely be able to figure out a vampire *murder*. He probably just wanted an excuse to see why you were in the city."

I held out my hand, sensing a familiar vampire

coming near, and I wished Steifan had not chosen now to start this conversation. Asher had probably heard every word.

Steifan reached for his sword, not understanding my silent warning.

I turned and looked back the way we'd come. Asher now stood roughly twenty paces away, having approached us as silent as only the dead can manage.

Steifan visibly relaxed, which was unnerving. One should never relax around a vampire.

"Did you find it?" I asked as Asher moved near us at human speed.

He produced a small, leather-bound journal from within his coat pocket.

My heart skipped a beat. Could it possibly be this easy? Would we find the answers to Charlotte's murder tonight?

Asher reached us, but did not offer the journal.

"Was it difficult to find?" I asked.

"No, the husband had already found it. He was preparing to burn it when I arrived."

"Did you kill him?" Steifan blurted.

Asher glared, and Steifan stepped back. I found myself glad to not be on the other end of that silver glare.

The vampire turned back to me. "I was forced to bespell the man. I tried to question him, but his mind proved surprisingly strong. I hope this will hold the answers you seek." He lifted the journal in his hand.

I reached for it, but he pulled it away.

"Give it to me," I demanded.

"Promise me that after this murder is solved, you will help me discover who killed the ancient."

I lowered my hand. There was no use trying to snatch anything from a vampire. "I can make no such promises. I follow the Potentate's orders, and he may have another mission for me."

He dangled the journal just out of reach above my head. "I don't think you follow anyone's orders, Lyssandra."

I put my hands on my hips, refusing to jump for the journal like a fool. "You know, people keep saying that to me."

"Promise me," he repeated, "and the journal is yours."

I frowned. I didn't like promising him anything, but I was already planning on looking into the murder. How could I not? "Fine," I hissed. "I promise."

He extended the journal to me and I snatched it away, clutching it against my chest. "I would thank you, but I don't want to, so for tonight, we are done. Where will I find you when I am ready to look into your murder?"

He looked up at the stars visible between the roofs on either side of the alley. "I believe I will spend some time within the city. I see no reason to waste such a long journey." He turned and strolled back down the alley.

Steifan moved to my side as I watched Asher fade

into the darkness. "Yeah, he definitely came here just to see you."

I wrinkled my nose. "Shut up, Steifan."

His laughter followed me as I retreated down the alley, making my way back toward the inn. As annoyed as I was, I was also excited to read the journal. When you needed to solve a murder, the mind of the victim was usually the best place to start.

I SAT ON THE WOODEN FLOOR OF OUR INN ROOM, A flickering lantern near my curled up knee. On my other side sat Steifan, leaning over to peer at the journal in my lap. No, not a journal, a ledger. In rows were scrawled names, locations, and numerical amounts. Unfortunately most of the names and locations were abbreviated, but at least the dates at the start of each new page were clear. We had taken off our armor to sit more comfortably, and had flipped through every page.

The ledger went back months, the final day taking place two weeks ago.

"Do you think this is a record of her," Steifan hesitated, "trade contacts?"

I smirked. "That's a pleasant way of putting it, but we don't even know if that rumor is true. What we do know is that this ledger was filled out nearly to the day she died." I pulled my braid from being trapped between my back and the edge of the bed we leaned against.

"How do you know which day she died? I assumed it was not as the duke claimed judging by the smell . . . "

I smiled, glad he'd noticed. "I know mostly from the smell, and the fact that she was moved. Lady Montrant claims she ended her friendship with Charlotte two weeks ago. That is about as long as it would take for a body to get to that stage of decomposition if it was left in a place warmer than the duke's estate."

"Why do you think the duke is lying about her death?" he asked.

I shrugged, still looking down at the abbreviated names in the ledger. "Who can say? I think he saw the bites on her neck and figured calling us here would be a good way to cover up what really happened. We would see the bites, hunt down the vampire, and the murder would be solved."

"So he didn't count on us actually having brains," Steifan said caustically.

I laughed. "It is not an uncommon assumption. We are warriors, not scholars."

Grinning, he gestured down to the ledger. "So what do we do with this?"

I lifted the book and flipped to the final filled-out page. "Just two names on this page. If she made these meetings, they might have been the last two people to see her alive. Tomorrow we try to find them."

Steifan read the page. "Well I'm not sure how we will locate S.D., but I recognize the second name, J. DeRose. At least I recognize the surname."

I tilted my head. "Odd, that she would mention a surname when most other names are abbreviated. Do you know any DeRoses in Silgard?"

He cringed. "The DeRose family probably has around one hundred living members, fifty or so of which dwell in the city. Ignoring the children, maybe twenty-five."

"And how many with the first initial J?" I asked.

"I could not say, but I imagine Bastien will know. The DeRoses are a prominent family."

I gave the ledger one last look, then shut it. "So tomorrow we will search for J. DeRose. We should get some rest now while we can."

He lifted a brow. "No more hunting vampires? I assumed you would want to go back out."

I stood. "Asher claims there are many vampires within the city, we may find one or two, but the chances of finding the one who bit Charlotte are slim. Now that the ledger has provided us with more to go on, I would rather rest, then pursue more likely angles tomorrow."

Still seated leaning against the bed, Steifan looked up at me. "Do you think Asher could figure out which vampire bit her?"

I tossed the ledger on the foot of the bed, then retrieved the sheathed Seeing Sword where I had left it on the ground beside me. "Even if he could, I would not ask him."

"But you asked him to steal the ledger."

I leaned the sword against the head of the bed where I could easily reach it if we were awakened. "He wouldn't be able to find the vampire," I sighed. "A bite on a dead woman is not much to go on. Normally when a body turns up, we can hunt the area and find the vampire's flock. But there are no territory lines here. We cannot pin a death to a certain flock just judging by the location. And like I said, I'm not sure the bite is what killed her."

He stood and straightened his shirt. "But if Asher could help, you would ask him?"

I narrowed my eyes. "I asked him tonight, did I not? His presence may vex me, but I would not put that above solving this murder."

He held up his hands in surrender. "My apologies, I did not mean to imply as such."

"And you will do well to not trust him either," I forged on. "I may be his human servant, but to him, you are just food. Do not let down your guard around him, nor any vampire."

Steifan fetched the lantern from the ground, then moved around the bed to set it on the windowsill. "Believe as you like, but I'm quite sure he won't harm me, because I am important to you."

I flopped down on the bed, nestling the back of my head against a pillow. "Every part of that sentence is irritating to me."

He walked to his side of the bed and plopped down beside me. "Are you more irritated that I am important to you, or that Asher so obviously cares?"

There was no way I was answering either of those

questions. "Remember when I told you to be careful around Asher?" I asked evenly.

"Yes, that was only moments ago."

I smiled sourly up at the ceiling. "Well you should be even more careful around me, I'm just as likely to tear your heart out."

He laughed, then got up to extinguish the lantern.

I shook my head, smiling in the sudden darkness. Steifan really believed I wouldn't tear out his heart. Maybe I was going soft.

Chapter Six

As promised, Bastien met us in the square an hour after dawn. I almost didn't recognize him without the duke's showy livery.

I said as much as he approached where we stood just outside the inn.

Looking down at his boots, he tugged the hem of his tan tunic. "I reckoned you'd not like me drawing any extra stares."

I realized I'd embarrassed him, and it really was smart for him to dress in less conspicuous clothing. His tunic and breeches, while well-made, were unremarkable. He did not stand out in the markets, nor would he be noticeable amongst peasants. He would obviously still be recognized in the White Quarter, but there it would not matter as much. There everyone already knew what we were looking for.

"You did good," I said. I glanced at Steifan, wondering where to begin.

We'd both had similar thoughts to Bastien on our clothing. I wore a midnight blue silk shirt and black leggings, while Steifan wore clothing nearly the twin of Bastien's. While we were supposed to wear our armor with its insignia at all times on a mission, we were far from Castle Helius, and we might gain more answers if people didn't realize we were hunters.

Our swords and extra weaponry might still stand out, but most would think us mercenaries.

I turned back to Bastien. "How much time can you spare us today?"

He grinned. "I have the rest of the day off. Vannier requested I do whatever it takes to help you find the monster who killed Duchess Auclair."

My eyebrows shot up. Odd, that it was the servant pushing for justice rather than the husband.

I glanced around the market, making sure no one paid us too much attention as I wondered how to broach the subject of J. DeRose with Bastien. By now the duke would have realized the ledger was missing, unless he simply woke up thinking he'd already burned it. Regardless, it was better to exercise caution and not let Bastien know we had the ledger.

Seeming to realize my predicament, Steifan looked around me to Bastien. "For our first task, can you guide us to the DeRoses? My father requested we pay several notable families a visit, and I'm not sure where this particular family dwells."

Bastien's expression fell. "I fear the DeRoses have gone out of favor. They fell victim to criminal activities and went destitute."

Steifan and I locked gazes for a moment. Why would Charlotte be meeting with a family that had fallen out of favor?

"Is there a particular member of the family you were tasked to approach?" Bastien asked hopefully.

Steifan's bashful expression was almost believable. "My father only gave me a list, and did not fully explain the names. At the top of the list was J. DeRose."

Bastien nodded, easily accepting the explanation. "That would be Jeramy DeRose. I know the general area of where he now lives," he paused, his eyes flicking me. "It is not an area for a proper lady to be seen."

Steifan snorted, earning him a deathly glare. I turned back to Bastien before I could ensure I had wiped the grin off Steifan's face. "I will be fine. Can you take us there?"

Bastien glanced at the Seeing Sword. "Yes, I do suppose you can take care of yourself. This way."

We followed as he cut across the square, opposite the direction of the stables. He led us down a narrow dirt street bisecting small wooden homes, some with shattered windows, and some that never had glass to begin with. Occasionally we heard voices from within the homes, most seeming to belong to mothers and children, though sometimes a man's voice was thrown in. These were probably the families of smiths, tailors, tavern workers, and the like. Farmers and peasants would live outside the city walls.

We followed the interior curve of those walls now, as the homes slowly fell to disrepair. Eventually they were little more than shacks, the planks oddly spaced enough to barely keep out the elements. Thatched roofs were mostly rotted, with some gone entirely, showing the wooden supports beneath.

There were more people out in the street here, some sleeping in the open beneath ragged piles of bedding. Two dirty, but healthy looking young men watched us closely as we passed. I didn't miss the way their eyes lingered on mine and Steifan's weapons, probably wondering if they would be able to take them from us.

Bastien stuck close to my shoulder as we continued on. "We will need to ask someone, I don't know exactly where Jeramy ended up."

My nose wrinkled at a familiar odor amidst the bouquet of unwashed bodies and excrement. "Perhaps, but let's check this way first."

I veered right after passing a vacant home, with Bastien and Steifan close behind. The smell grew worse. I was getting a bad feeling.

Just as I thought it, the Seeing Sword thrummed at my back.

I increased my pace.

Realizing something was wrong, Steifan jogged to keep up at my side, but didn't ask questions.

We came to a small cul-de-sac of homes. A young mother watched us from across the way, her children playing in the dirt at her feet. Her eyes flicked to a house directly across from hers, which seemed to be the one harboring the horrid stench.

Bastien and Steifan each lifted a sleeve to cover their noses, so it must have been strong enough now for them to smell it too.

"I really don't like the smell of this," Steifan groaned.

"It might have nothing to do with J. DeRose," I said, already walking toward the home. The young mother had gathered her children and retreated through her door.

I reached the odor harboring door with the Seeing Sword thrumming steadily at my back. I listened for a moment, then braced my right leg, flicking out the other to kick the door in.

It flew back with a loud *thwack*, then fell partially off its hinges. The smell was overwhelming. I covered my nose and mouth with my sleeve and walked inside.

A man lay sprawled in the middle of the floor, his body ripe with the hot sunlight streaming in through the damaged roof. Rusty brown stains had soaked into the hard-packed dirt floor. The straw mat and few belongings within the home had been tossed about, some things torn to shreds.

I sensed Steifan and Bastien at my back as I knelt near the putrid corpse. It was difficult to tell with the mottled skin, but it seemed like he had been badly beaten before being killed. I picked up a fallen quill to move light brown hair away from his neck. No vampire bites, though that didn't mean they weren't elsewhere on his body.

"I think that's Jeramy," Bastien croaked behind me.

I turned to see him staring wide-eyed at the corpse. His skin had gone so pale, his freckles stood out like ink stains.

"Are you sure?" I asked.

Bastien's body convulsed like he might vomit. He clamped a hand over his mouth and nodded.

"Wait for us outside," I instructed. "Do not go far, and yell if anyone bothers you." Once he was gone, I looked to Steifan. "What do you think?"

I asked it like I already knew what he should think, but in truth I hadn't a clue.

While he looked a little green, Steifan maintained his composure. "I think that our only lead is dead, though I cannot tell the cause of death."

I stood and took a step away from the corpse. "The patterns on his flesh would suggest strangling after a long period of physical violence. Yet the stains on the floor suggest a large amount of blood was spilled here."

Steifan observed the darker stains on the dirt floor. "Do you think . . . Charlotte?"

I looked back down at the corpse, willing it to tell me its secrets. "Perhaps. Her neck wound wouldn't have been enough for so much blood, and that would mean a vampire didn't drink it. We should have checked the back of her body for other wounds." I shook my head, feeling like the idiot that I was. "I don't go into situations considering that mortals would actually fake a vampire kill. Perhaps I should start. Our carelessness has deprived us of answers."

Bastien's raised voice caught my ear. "It would be unwise of you to quarrel with my associates!"

I was rushing outside before I could even think about it. Once I saw the four men surrounding Bastien, and they saw me, the Seeing Sword echoed a warning. As if I couldn't already tell that these criminals meant us harm.

Steifan was at my back, both of us yet to draw our swords.

Our would-be assailants took measure of us. They hardly merited the same in return, but the one with a crudely made blade was too close to Bastien. He could slit Bastien's throat before we could reach him.

I took a few slow steps toward the group, and the men did not react. Good. If I could get close enough, I could eliminate the threat before Bastien could be harmed.

"We probably don't want to kill them," Steifan whispered behind me.

"I'm not an idiot," I hissed, then more loudly asked, "What do you want?"

The man with the blade spun it like he knew how to use it. "Your swords, and perhaps a taste of your lovely flesh, witch."

Bastien seemed frozen beside him, unsure of what to do. Two of the other men had swords riding their shoulders. Muscles corded down their tanned arms, with white scars standing in stark relief. The older of the pair had a wicked scar across one eye.

I took another step closer. "Well you can't have my sword, and my flesh is out of the question, so I might just take a *slice* of yours instead."

The man closest to Bastien laughed. "Come and get it, witch."

I drew the Seeing Sword, but Steifan was right, we needed to avoid killing them. Wouldn't do to have word spread that hunters were killing *innocent* people, because that's exactly what witnesses would say if they figured out what we were.

The men eyed my sword hungrily. I heard Steifan's sword hiss from its sheath.

With all eyes on our swords, I swiftly moved one hand from my hilt and drew a dagger from my belt, sending it sailing toward the man near Bastien.

It sliced across his arm, as intended, missing anything vital. But his momentary surprise gave me the time I needed to lunge forward and shove Bastien out of the way. As Bastien hit the dirt, I turned, lifting my sword to parry a strike from the scar-faced swordsman. I spun my sword in a small circle, catching his blade and tossing it aside.

He looked at me in shock, like he'd never had

someone disarm him before, and maybe he hadn't. He preyed on the weak. I would have loved to kill him.

He saw his own death in my eyes, and slowly backed away, hands raised.

Steifan had disarmed the other swordsman, and the man who had originally threatened Bastien clutched his bleeding arm, his blade nowhere to be seen. The fourth man, who had never shown a weapon, was backing away, on the edge of fleeing and leaving his partners behind.

With the situation fully assessed, I whipped my blade back toward the scar-faced swordsman, aiming the tip at his throat.

He lifted his hands again. "You win, no amount of coin is worth this."

I edged my sword's tip a little closer to his throat. The sword was quiet, he meant what he said, yet his words confused me. "What do you mean? What coin?"

His voice came out strained, "A stranger approached me with a lot of coin. Said to gather some of my boys and keep an eye out for a red-haired witch."

I pressed my sword against his flesh. "Did the stranger tell you to kill me?"

He gulped, drawing a pinprick of blood on his throat. "Yes, and anyone with you. But it's not worth the coin to me anymore, I swear it."

"What did the stranger look like?"

He shook his head minutely. "Don't know, it was dark, he wore a hood. He gave me half the coin upfront, and said he would find me with the rest once you were dead."

I smiled wickedly, debating killing him regardless of the consequences. Anyone who would take coin to kill an innocent stranger deserved to die.

"Please don't kill me," he rasped.

"Lyss," Steifan's voice was low with warning.

I lowered my blade, my attention still on the man before me. "You will leave the city, and you will never look back. If I ever catch a glimpse of you again, you will become the hunted. For I am of the Helius Order. Hunting is what I do best."

His bulging eyes and gaping jaw told me the stranger had not informed him we were hunters. Now that he knew, he would not be bothering us again. But still, if I ever saw him outside of the city, somewhere private, I would finish what I had started. Because I knew he would go on to harm someone else.

He took two steps back, then turned and ran, leaving his sword in the dirt.

Steifan brandished his blade at the other three men, and they all turned tail and scurried away.

Once we were alone, Bastien ran toward me. "That was amazing! You saved my life!"

"No," I said, my gaze on Jeramy's broken door, "I nearly got you killed. I want you to go back to the duke's estate. Do not approach us again."

"But—"

"Go!" I shouted.

Bastien aimed the full weight of his hurt expression at me for a heartbeat, then turned and ran away.

Steifan moved to my side, watching him go. "You didn't have to be so harsh."

I sheathed my sword, then picked up my dagger from the dirt. "There have been two murders, and someone wants them to go unsolved enough to hire mercenaries to kill us. They could have killed Bastien before we even stepped outside. If anything, I was not harsh enough. He needs to stay away."

Steifan sighed and sheathed his sword. "What do we do now?"

"We find anyone involved in Charlotte's murder, and we cut off their heads." I started walking. If I wasn't on a warpath before, I most certainly was now.

Chapter Seven

We headed back toward the inn in silence. I wanted to make sure our few belongings and horses were safe before venturing back toward the White Quarter. If someone had been hired to kill us, someone else might have been hired to make off with our horses and goods to cover up our disappearance.

The Seeing Sword was steadily making my spine itch with its energy as we walked, but it was hard to tell who was pondering attacking me. Many eyes watched us from within hovels and out on the street. Word of our altercation had spread quickly.

I took another step, then nearly stumbled as a strange sensation passed over me, like walking through quicksand.

Steifan kept walking, not seeming to notice anything amiss. He didn't even notice as he left me further and further behind. My steps slowed until I could no longer lift my feet. The eyes on either side of the street followed Steifan, none looking my way.

I felt oddly not real, and it was a sensation I recognized. It was broad daylight, so it wasn't vampire mind tricks. It was glamour. Glamour so strong it made my mind believe I couldn't move. Even though I knew it was happening, I couldn't fight it.

I wasn't surprised when I heard the Nattmara's voice behind me. "Hello hunter, I did not expect to see you this far from Castle Helius."

I turned to face Egar, the male Nattmara who'd escaped us in Charmant. He was also part Sidhe, which was why no one in the streets seemed able to see us. Now that Steifan was out of sight, many of them retreated to their homes.

"I saw you yesterday, didn't I?" I asked. "I saw you beyond a fence in a garden." The face I had seen was clear to me now, the short dark hair and large blue eyes. I hadn't wanted to believe it was him.

Egar inclined his clean-shaven chin. He looked young and harmless, though I knew he was anything but. "I smelled a corpse. I wanted to collect it, but you beat me there."

I nearly gagged at the thought of Egar eating Charlotte's rotted corpse. "I thought Nattmara preferred fresh victims."

He licked his lips. "Yes, but any will do. All I need is flesh and blood to sustain me. I like to get to know my environment before I start hunting, and I only just arrived here yesterday."

I considered the possibility of Egar being Charlotte's killer, and perhaps seeking out her corpse to finish feeding, but it didn't add up. If he'd had her and maybe even Jeramy freshly dead, we would have found little more than bones and globs of flesh.

"What do you want from me, Egar? You know now that I've found you, I will have to kill you."

He laughed, a young, charming sound that fit his exterior. The worst of monsters were usually just dark on the inside. "You are trying to solve a murder. I could tell you what you're missing."

He was standing so close he could reach out and strangle me, and I would be powerless to stop him. Every muscle in my body strained to move, but it was hopeless. "You claim to have just arrived yesterday. What could you possibly know?"

His satisfied grin told me he hadn't just arrived, and he had lied about what he'd been doing among the wealthy estates. "I know a lot of things, hunter. I know that there is powerful blood within the city, far more delicious than yours. Help me find it, and I will help you solve your murder."

"You know I would not sacrifice another human to you. Now free me from this glamour, I have much to do."

He tilted his head. "I thought you wanted to kill me. Now you simply want to escape?"

I sucked my teeth. That, and moving my mouth was

all I could manage. I was lucky he was allowing air into my lungs. I did want to kill him, he deserved to die, but I knew I wasn't capable. I wanted to draw my sword, but my arms didn't budge. If he wanted to kill me right now, he could probably just cloud my mind and I'd be dead before I realized what was happening.

He watched the thoughts play across my face. "I see you understand. My sister was powerful, but she inherited mostly my mother's blood. I have the glamour of the Sidhe, and no mortal can stand against it. I believe you will be drawn to the powerful blood in this city like a moth to the flame, or else it will be drawn to you." He stepped closer. "I will be watching you, hunter. You will lead me to what I want, and if you don't, I'll take you instead. You should have let me help you solve your murder while you had the chance."

Reality seemed to shift, sending me reeling backward. When I righted myself, I was alone in the street.

"Lyss!" Steifan shouted.

I turned to see him running toward me.

He grabbed my arms as he reached me. "Where did you go? I was nearly back to the inn when I realized you weren't beside me."

"The Nattmara was here." I shook my head, what were the chances that I would run into that creature again? "It is hunting something here."

Steifan let me go. "Egar?"

"Yes." I felt badly shaken. I had faced powerful beings, but not like Egar. How could you kill something that could warp your mind so completely? The death of Egar's father, the one who had kept him contained, was going to be the death of us all.

Steifan looked me over, slowly shaking his head. "I've never seen you like this, Lyss."

"Like what?" I asked distantly.

"Scared."

A few people had come out into the street to watch us. Despite the sun shining overhead, my skin felt cold. "Let's get out of here. We need a pint of ale and a new plan. We must figure out how to kill the Nattmara."

As we started walking, I noticed Steifan glancing around warily, as if he expected the Nattmara to still be watching us. Maybe he was, but as long as I wasn't under the creature's glamour, the Seeing Sword should warn me. In fact, Egar was probably the reason the sword had whispered a few warnings while we were in the wealthy district. And maybe even the reason Steifan thought he felt eyes on him.

"How can we kill it, Lyss?" Steifan asked, breaking the drawn out silence.

"I don't know. Most of what is known about Nattmara is little more than myth. We are probably some of the only people alive today to have faced one."

Steifan was quiet for a moment, but I could tell he had something to say.

I kept my attention trained on the street around us as we neared the nicer homes leading back to the market square. "What is it?"

"Asher is an ancient. He might know something about Nattmara. He might even be able to kill it. Does glamour work on vampires?"

I sighed. Now that the shock had worn off, I was beginning to get angry. We were here to solve a murder— two murders now—I did *not* need the issue of the Nattmara added to the list. "I don't know. I don't know anything anymore, but the Nattmara is not the only thing in the city that wants our blood. We must move forward with caution."

"Should we leave the inn?"

It wasn't a bad idea. Surely once the mysterious stranger realized we were still alive, someone else would be hired. We might be attacked in a more public place where we would be forced to kill someone. "I don't know where we would go." I stopped walking and looked to him. We were nearly at the square. "Do you have any connections you could use? Find us a place to stay, and a place to stable the horses?"

His hazel eyes danced with worry. "I might be able to find us somewhere, but we would be endangering any who would take us in."

He was right. We could not ask innocent people to harbor us. "We'll have to find somewhere on our own. There are plenty of warehouses in the city. If you could find someone to stable our horses, that should be safe enough."

"Consider it done."

We were drawing a few eyes, so we continued walking. I didn't like feeling so vulnerable, far away from Castle Helius and other hunters. I knew Steifan would watch my back, but it might not be enough. I might just have to take his suggestion and ask a certain vampire for help.

Did glamour work on vampires? We would soon find out.

Chapter Eight

By nightfall Steifan had found a place to stable our horses with our few extra belongings, and I had learned some interesting information. Talk of the tavern was that there was a witch practicing within the city. Real witches were extremely rare, so she probably wasn't genuine . . . but if she was real, she might know how to break Egar's glamour.

It was worth investigating, mostly because we didn't have any other options. Maybe she would even have insight on the missing people. Of course, she could also be the murderer. According to the histories, the most powerful spells often required sacrifices, the closer to human, the better.

Steifan and I walked north, passing the wrought iron gate to the wealthy estates without stopping. We had provided enough pints of ale to learn that the witch could be found in the old part of the city where the former keep once stood, long abandoned since a new keep had been erected within the White Quarter.

The road we walked wound ever upward toward the apex of the hill upon which the city was built. We left the light of torches and lamps behind for the more subtle glow of occasional candles in windows and a few distant fires. These darker streets were the perfect haunt for pickpockets, yet somehow I felt safer in the darkness. More hidden and at peace.

The old wall came into view, casting deeper shadows in the darkness. Parts of the wall had been toppled during the siege that had taken place well before the borders of the Ebon Province had been drawn.

There were fewer people in this part of the city, but we did catch occasional glances from beyond open shutters, evidenced only by a shadow darting away as soon as it caught our attention. A young couple hurried down the road toward us, giving us a wary glance as they passed by. Judging by their clothing, they were rushing back to a rich estate, and judging by their pace, they were fearful of being robbed now that darkness had fallen. I briefly wondered what they were doing in this part of the city to begin with, then cast the thought aside as we neared the old keep, and the small nomadic civilization that had sprung up around it.

My eyes searched across flickering lanterns and small fires. Clusters of people shared pots of soup and loaves of bread while sitting near covered wagons and stacks of crates.

"This must be where traveling merchants and caravans come to stay," I said to Steifan as we stopped walking.

"And other sorts," he added, eyeing a pair leaning against a nearby wall in dark cloaks, their faces lost in shadow. They had no visible weapons, but instinct alone told me they were not to be trifled with.

We kept walking, observing the small camps while keeping our ears open for mention of the witch.

A young woman hurried out the gaping doorway of an ancient stone home. She clutched a wrapped bundle against her chest, her eyes shifting around nervously. Scented smoke wafted from within the home, which glowed with flickering firelight.

I stopped across the street from the home as the nervous young woman scurried off into the night. "Something tells me we've found what we're looking for."

A merchant sitting near a fire to our right looked up at us. "If you're searching for the witch, you have found the place. But be wary, those dwelling in these parts are protective of her."

I nodded my thanks. "I assure you, we mean her no harm."

A little thrill of excitement trickled up my spine. If these people would protect her, maybe she was a real witch, and a helpful one at that. Just as witches could curse and maim, they could also heal. This might very well be the only chance Steifan and I would have to meet one. If she could help us with the Nattmara, then all the better.

I led the way across the street and looked into the open doorway.

The woman sitting cross-legged in front of the fire was already looking up at me. Her dark eyes, like flecks of onyx set into a pale face, matched her long black hair. She appeared young, I would guess around twenty, and wore a long white dress that looked almost like a night shift.

She watched me warily. "I sensed someone coming, but I did not expect a hunter. Why are you here?"

I stepped through the doorway, making room for Steifan. The feel of magic made me catch my breath. This place was strongly warded, and I knew instantly I had only been able to step inside because she let me.

I swallowed the lump in my throat. "How could you tell I was a hunter?" We had intentionally left our armor with our horses, not wanting the witch to believe we had come to kill her.

She seemed small huddled behind her fire, the yellow light giving her an ethereal look. "I can sense what you are, just as much as I can sense what he is not." She bobbed her chin toward Steifan.

Did that mean she could sense that I was a vampire's human servant? I didn't have the nerve to ask. "Are you really a witch?"

She bared her teeth. "Some say I am. What is it to you?"

It seemed I had angered her. *Wonderful.* A witch cursing me on top of everything else was all I needed. "We are here to ask for your help. Something hunts us, and we do not know how to defeat it."

She stood, and she was just as small standing up as I had imagined. "The hunters are the hunted? How poetic."

I was getting the feeling that she wasn't fond of hunters. If she was a real witch, I couldn't blame her. While we had stopped hunting witches decades ago, there was a time when we killed them as indiscriminately as vampires.

I glanced at Steifan, who shrugged. He wasn't quite sure what to make of this woman either. Staying any longer was a risk, but . . .

"Look," I said, stepping toward the fire, "I have never harmed a witch, in fact I have never met one. Any quarrel we might have is between our ancestors, not us."

She stepped up opposite me on the other side of the fire, so that we mirrored each other over the flames. "Does our ancestors blood not run through our veins? Have hunters ever paid us reparations?"

She had me there. "If you cannot help us, we will leave you in peace." I stepped back. If she wasn't going to help us, I'd rather not make her angry. There was no telling how powerful she might be.

Suddenly she smiled, and it lit her entire face. "A

hunter willing to back down, how refreshing. What is your name?"

"Lyssandra," I answered, hesitating.

"I am Ryllae. What is it you would like help with?"

Her sudden change in mood had me grasping for words. Finally, I managed to ask, "You were testing me, weren't you?"

"Can you blame me?"

I shrugged. "I suppose one cannot be too careful. Does this mean you'll answer my questions now?"

"It means we will trade information. You have many secrets, Lyssandra."

"Lyss," Steifan interrupted. "Some secrets might not be worth sharing."

He was right. She had already implied that I was different from Steifan. If she wanted to know what I was, I would be a fool to tell her. If she sold me out to the wrong person, it could get me killed.

Of course, it wouldn't matter much if Egar killed me first. I recalled the sensation of him clouding my mind, how helpless I was standing before him, and my decision was made.

I stared into Ryllae's dark eyes. "Fine, if you tell me what I need to know, I will share whatever secret you wish, but *only* if you have the answers I seek."

She inclined her head. "A fair trade. Now ask your question."

I glanced at Steifan, buying time. If I was only going to get one question, I needed to make it count. And when it came to Egar, only one question really mattered. I turned my attention back to Ryllae. "Do you know anything of glamour? How to break it?"

"You are hoping to slay the Nattmara," she observed.

"You know of it?" Steifan asked, stepping up beside me.

She crossed her arms and shivered, though the fire in the small space had me sweating. "It hunts me too. It has not managed to find me yet, but I fear it will eventually."

Could she be the powerful blood the Nattmara had mentioned? It would make sense. "You're afraid of it," I observed.

"I have been hiding since it arrived in the city, watching it when I can. It seeks me tirelessly."

"You were not so difficult to find, you do realize that?"

She smiled. "You found me because I wished you to find me. I knew it was a risk, but I needed to see if you could be trusted."

"And can I?"

"You were prepared to leave me when I would not cooperate," she explained. "That alone lets me know I can trust you. You are not working with the creature. Anyone working with that thing would have tried to force answers from me."

"Do you know how to break his glamour?"

Her arms still wrapped tightly around her, she raised dark brows. "If I knew, do you believe you could kill it?"

"I slew the creature's sister in a small village in the North. She had hoped to feast on my blood."

She finally lowered her arms, her surprise clear. "Did the sister not share in his glamour?"

"Their father was part Sidhe, and the mother pure-blooded Nattmara. The sister took after their mother, but Egar strongly inherited his father's gifts. The father was keeping them both contained until he was killed."

She looked down into the fire. "This explains much. The creature has nearly broken through my glamour many times. I hadn't previously understood how he would possess such gifts."

"Do witches really know glamour?" Steifan asked.

Her lips curled into the barest of smiles. "No child, I never said I was a witch, only that others believe it to be so."

My jaw fell open as realization threatened. Suddenly it made sense how a witch could survive in the middle of the city. How she could only be found by those she chose. If she could do glamour, she could hide in plain sight. But witches couldn't do real glamour. Only one type of creature could. "You're Sidhe, aren't you?"

Steifan balked at me, but I was pretty sure I was right. This was why the Nattmara wanted her blood so badly. It could potentially sustain him for centuries.

She watched me for a moment, then nodded.

"So you know how to break his glamour?" I pressed, stepping close enough to the fire that my toes grew hot through the leather of my boots.

"Yes, but there is one problem. You are hunters, and you may someday hunt me. If I tell you how to break the Nattmara's glamour, you may be able to break mine as well."

I shook my head. "We have no reason to harm you. The people of this area protect you. It seems you live a life of peace."

She watched me for a long moment, and I almost thought our slim chance of defeating Egar was slipping through my fingers. Seeming to come to a decision, she said, "I will tell you, but my price still stands. There is a secret to you, something you hide. It makes you different from him." She gestured to Steifan. "Tell me what it is, then I will decide whether or not I will help you with the Nattmara."

My stomach seemed to turn over completely within me. I had spoken this secret three times now, but no time had been any easier than the prior.

"Ask something else," Steifan interjected. "Anything else."

I turned to him.

"We have only just met her," he pleaded. "This secret can be a danger to you. If she tells anyone . . ."

"I am well aware of the danger, but we cannot leave Egar alive. He will kill many, and he will eventually kill us." My mind made up, I turned back to the woman who had already shared a dangerous secret with us. I had to trust her. "I am a vampire's human servant. If the Helius Order were to find out, I would be executed. If you can

tell us how to break the Nattmara's glamour, I will take
your secret to the grave."

Her dark eyes scrutinized me. She took a long slow
breath, then exhaled. "I will teach you, and only you. You
will share this with no one, not even him." Her eyes
flicked to Steifan, then back to me. "And we will swear an
oath, we will take each other's secrets to the grave. As a
hunter you should know what it means to swear an oath
to one of the Sidhe."

I did know. I knew that if I betrayed her, the spirits
of her ancestors would haunt me for eternity. But I would
take the risk if it meant slaying the Nattmara. "I will take
your oath, and together we will defeat our enemy."

She smiled then, another real smile that lit up her
face. "Send your companion outside and we will get
started."

"Lyss, think about this," Steifan cautioned. "She has
glamour too. She's dangerous."

I placed my hand on his shoulder and gave an encour-
aging squeeze. "Egar intends to kill me eventually. I
cannot wait around for that to happen. I must learn to
break his glamour."

He looked to Ryllae. "If you harm her—"

She smiled indulgently, like one would at a child. It
made me wonder just how old she was. "I will only harm
her if she harms me. If her intentions are pure, she is
safe. Do not fear."

He didn't look like he quite believed her, but he
squeezed my hand on his shoulder, then turned away. He

walked out into the night, leaving us alone in the small stone space.

I turned back to Ryllae.

"You'll really kill the Nattmara?" she asked.

I smiled and answered honestly. "It would be my pleasure."

Chapter Nine

I guessed it was sometime around midnight when I finally emerged from Ryllae's home. I had already sensed what I would find outside, and my eyes confirmed it. Asher waited with Steifan, both leaning against a portion of wall near a merchant camp. Seeing me, they headed in my direction.

Ryllae walked out and stood beside me, following my gaze. "*Oh*, now I see why you don't want to kill him." Her mischievous smile said she knew exactly who Asher was to me, and she approved of what she saw, at least physically. I knew from our conversation she held no love for vampires, especially ancient ones.

"I never said I didn't want to kill him," I grumbled as the men neared. "Just that I'm not going to kill him quite yet."

"You are an honest woman, Lyssandra. It would be a

shame if you continued to go against your nature by lying to yourself."

I frowned as Asher and Steifan reached us, wishing I had been a little less honest with the woman at my side. I'd felt I had owed it to her to answer her seemingly harmless questions when she was sharing with me the most closely guarded secret of her people.

Said secret wasn't as complex as I had thought it would be. All it required was a resilient mind, an ancient chant, and enough power to back it up, which she swore I had, though I was doubtful. The jar of ointment she had given me would be supplementary. I could put it on my eyes and ears to block out visual and auditory glamour. The ointment was for Steifan too, but the bit of chanting and magic was just for me.

"What are you doing here?" I asked Asher.

But he was looking at Ryllae. "Not a witch after all," he said. "How interesting."

Ryllae's eyes flared at his words. Suddenly she seemed bigger than the tiny woman she was. She took a step toward Steifan. "You told him."

Steifan held up his hands. "I did no such thing!"

A few onlookers still awake sitting around fires glanced our way like they might interfere.

"I can smell your blood," Asher said lowly. "I have known your kind before. No one has betrayed your secret, nor will I."

Ryllae stepped back like he had struck her. "My kind? Where? When?"

Sorrow stabbed my gut. I looked at Asher and saw that sorrow echoed in his expression. I stared at him, unsure where my sudden emotions had come from.

"It was many centuries ago," he said to Ryllae. "I apologize if I gave you false hope."

I moved to stand closer to Steifan, further from the vampire. Had I actually just felt his emotions? Karpov had once told me that I would grow closer to Asher the more I was around him. Was that happening now?

I didn't have time to ask any questions, and now wasn't the time for it regardless.

Ryllae took a moment to process Asher's words. I wondered how long ago she had become separated from the last of her kin, and if any could possibly be alive.

She met my waiting gaze. "Remember what we discussed. Return to me when the Nattmara is dead." With that she turned and went back into her home.

I looked to Asher. "You never answered my question. Why are you here?"

"I will tell you, but not here." He gestured subtly to the men still watching us.

I met their waiting eyes, then nodded. The Seeing Sword had offered no warnings, the men meant us no harm, but it was best not to discuss anything near listening ears. The shock of feeling Asher's emotions had made me careless. I wouldn't let it happen again.

I looked around, then led the way toward the dark remains of the original keep. There were a few other fires in that direction, but more spread out. We should be able to find a private place to speak.

When the three of us were crowded into an alcove, far from any fires, I looked to Asher expectantly, angling my shoulder back so it wouldn't be touching his.

He smiled, finding me amusing. "I believe I may have learned something that will help in solving your murder. I began my evening near the home of the man you had me steal the journal from. I witnessed a servant exchanging coin with an unsavory type in the dark shadows of the gardens."

I crossed my arms, growing colder the longer I was away from Ryllae's fire. "What sort of unsavory type?"

"The type that carries a sword, has many scars, and bathes little. I followed him as far as I could, then picked up his scent later on near the inn. I attempted to check on your belongings, but it seems someone else now occupies your room."

I mulled over this new information before looking to Steifan. "You didn't tell him?"

Steifan shrugged, looking a little embarrassed. "I wasn't sure how much you wanted him to know."

I smiled, appreciating the gesture. "I suppose we were wise to move the horses."

Asher looked back and forth between us. "Would one of you mind telling me what you're talking about?"

I almost didn't want to tell him just to be petty, but he *had* brought us the information about the duke's servant, presumably Vannier, paying someone who looked like a mercenary. "We were attacked this morning," I explained. "A group of men was hired to kill us."

He went utterly still. Only the tendrils of his white hair slightly shifting broke the illusion that he was suddenly a statue. "Someone was paid to kill you?" he asked slowly.

"Why do you seem so surprised?"

His expression returned in the form of a scowl. "I am not surprised, I am outraged. For someone to not only mean you harm, but to be cowardly enough to not enact it himself? If the man I robbed of the journal is responsible, I will put an end to him."

I grabbed his arm, just in case he was thinking about going anywhere. "We don't know that it was him. Vannier, the duke's servant, could have been paying that man for any number of reasons. The duke wanted us here to investigate his wife's murder, I don't know why he would try to kill us."

"Unless we were getting too close," Steifan said. "He probably expected us just to come in and hunt a vampire."

"You're right," I conceded, letting go of Asher's arm. "He seemed surprised that we wanted to question her friends and read her journals, but that doesn't mean he tried to have us killed. Still, he is covering up something larger than his wife's murder, and we need to find out what that is."

Asher shifted a little closer to me as voices came near

our alcove, then faded away. "The Sidhe mentioned a Nattmara earlier. How is that related?"

Steifan really didn't tell him *anything*. I was so proud. "The Nattmara I slew in Charmant had a brother. Their father was Sidhe."

Asher's brow furrowed. "That is an unfortunate combination. A predator with gifts only a peaceful race like the Sidhe should possess."

I nodded. "And possess them he does. I encountered him earlier and he managed to control my mind to the point where I could not move. No one around could see us, and not even my sword could mutter a warning."

"And why have you only just encountered this creature recently?" Asher asked. "I imagine it would have been killing often."

I gave Steifan an apologetic look, knowing it was a sore subject for him, then answered, "His father had limited his powers, but unfortunately was killed."

"By me," Steifan added. "I freed the beast."

Asher barely acknowledged Steifan. He was still staring at me. "And you approached the Sidhe hoping for a way to limit the effects of glamour."

"You do catch on fast," I said. "And my hopes were answered, she taught me how to overcome the Nattmara's glamour. I can only hope I am strong enough."

"I would give much to learn what she told you. Yet because you're my servant, your mind is closed to me."

I snorted. "Well that is fortunate, isn't it? Because if I

told you, I'd have to kill you. And that would kill me too."

I noticed Steifan watching us with amusement and my mood soured. "Let's get out of here. I think it's time we paid Vannier a visit."

Both men nodded their agreement, and we left the alcove, heading back toward the newer part of the city.

In truth, the servant was probably the least of our worries, but we would focus on him while we could. I had no idea how to hunt down the Nattmara, but I knew soon enough, the Nattmara would be hunting *me*.

Chapter Ten

We walked along the wall bordering the estates in silence, with Asher on my left, and Steifan on my right. It seemed Asher would be joining us for the rest of the evening. I wasn't sure how I felt about that. At least there were no other hunters around to see me walking with a vampire.

It was late enough now that few people were out, so we were alone as we rounded a bend and the two guards posted in front of the wrought iron gates came into view. I stopped walking, then retreated out of sight, pressing my back against the wall. Steifan followed my movements like a normal human being, but Asher was like a shadow. As I moved, he moved, needing no time to catch up. It was horribly unnerving.

Steifan didn't seem to notice. He stood at my shoulder, leaning near to keep his voice low. "How are we going to get in? I doubt they'll believe we are going to visit the duke at this late hour."

I didn't want to admit that I hadn't even thought about the guards. Between the mercenaries, Egar, and Ryllae, it had been a long day.

Asher's silver eyes sparkled with moonlight as he leaned close to me and lowered his voice. "The man who met with the servant went through the canal beneath the wall. That is perhaps an option you would like to consider."

I blinked at him. "You followed him through an underground canal?"

He shook his head. "No, only to the entrance, as I wanted to keep an eye on the servant. I picked up the unsavory man's scent again after leaving the inn. There is a canal entrance behind the guild hall."

"And what were you doing at the inn?" I pressed.

"Looking for you. After that I followed your trail to where you stabled your horses, then to the Sidhe."

"My you've been busy," I said tersely.

"We should take to the canals then," Steifan interrupted pointedly, giving me a look which implied I should behave myself.

I would have argued, but he was right. If there was an underground way into the White Quarter, we should explore it. "Yes, back to the subject of the canals," I sighed, turning to Asher. Then my mind caught up with my mouth and my jaw fell open.

"You've had a realization," Asher observed.

I just shook my head, not in response to his question, but to my own stupidity. I knew the canals existed, but I hadn't considered them. "That's how they must have moved Charlotte's body. That's why it was wet."

Asher tilted his head. "Charlotte is the murdered woman? If one wanted to move a body through the canal, one might do so without getting wet."

Steifan nodded along. "But if she was killed with Jeramy, that would have been a long way to carry a body, especially if it was just one person carrying her. It would be easier to float the body through the water."

I looked back to Asher. "Can you show us the way into the canal?"

He gave a small bow. "As *my lady* wishes."

Steifan let out a soft chortle at my indignant expression, lifting a hand to his mouth to suppress the sound.

I glared at him as I turned to follow Asher.

The vampire led us away from the wall and out of sight from the guards, then south toward the guild hall not far from the inn. We circled the towering building, heading into a dead-end alcove with walls lending privacy on all sides. If Asher hadn't been looking for me at the inn, he might not have caught the man's scent in this out-of-the-way place.

Asher stopped walking and gestured toward a set of cellar doors. A steel chain wound several times between the handles, held in place by a padlock.

"I found the man's scent again here," he explained.

"The padlock also smells strongly of him. I imagine he had a set of keys."

I stared down at the thick steel chain. "Was the other end of the canal locked?"

He shook his head. "The man did not lock it upon his departure, but I cannot guarantee someone else did not lock it after I was gone."

"Couldn't you just have bespelled him or the servant?" Steifan asked. "It seems an awful lot of work to do things this way."

Asher gave him a less than friendly look. "You would be surprised how resilient the minds of some mortals can be. If I would have attempted to bespell the servant, there's a chance it would not have worked, then I would have needed to kill him. That seemed unnecessary."

Unnecessary, I thought. That was one way of putting it.

"But you bespelled the duke," Steifan pressed. "If it hadn't worked, would you have killed him?"

"Yes."

I gaped at him.

Asher lifted his nose. "Judge me if you will, Lyssandra. But I was only in such a situation because you asked me to go. It is not my fault you did not consider the possibilities."

I let out a long breath through my clenched teeth. "I suppose you're right." I had to be more careful what I asked for in the future. Turning away to hide my flushed cheeks, I gestured to the cellar doors. "Can you break the lock?"

Asher stepped up beside me. "As could you, I imagine."

"I might be able to break down doors, but I cannot bend steel."

"If you believe it to be so, then it must be so." With that annoyingly cryptic reply, he knelt, wrapped one hand around the chain, then tore it free with a loud groan of metal.

The handles on the cellar doors gave before the chain did, but it got the job done. Asher lifted one door open, revealing stairs leading down into darkness.

"What's that term," Steifan said at my opposite shoulder. "Ah yes, ladies first."

With a smug look, I marched down into the darkness. The Seeing Sword would warn me if there was any danger . . . I hoped. I reached the bottom of the short stone staircase, then could go no further. It was pitch black. I could feel the stone wall to my right, and could hear water flowing to my left. The cellar door creaked shut above as footsteps echoed down the stairs behind me.

I heard the distinct sound of flint grating on fire steel, then a lantern flared to life.

Asher shielded the lantern with one hand so as not to blind me. "I could smell the oil," he said, bobbing the lantern in his hand. Once my eyes had adjusted, he extended it to me.

"My thanks," I said through gritted teeth, finding it difficult to mutter my gratitude. I took the lantern handle, brushing his long, cool fingers with my skin. I suppressed a shiver. "Let's go."

We walked one by one down the narrow canal. Asher walked directly behind me, making me uneasy. I had been trained my entire life to never turn my back on a vampire, now here I was, willingly working with one. If only my uncle could see me now.

Supposedly following the man's scent, Asher spoke directions as we wound our way through the canals. They were like a maze. Anyone traveling this route would have to know the way well. It made me wonder just who had transported Charlotte's body.

"It is here," Asher said as we rounded a bend.

I extended the lantern to light the way ahead. Sure enough, a rickety metal ladder led up to a closed hatch.

I approached the ladder, then set the lantern on the stones near its base before climbing the bottom rung. "Is it just me, or is it odd for the canals to have these random entrances?"

Asher answered at my back. "After the siege where the old keep was destroyed, the canals were built. The nobles wanted a way to escape should the city fall under siege once again. Some of the outlets lead all the way outside the main wall. The easy access to water was a secondary concern."

I looped one elbow on a ladder rung, then leaned to look back at him. "So if the city were to fall under siege, the nobles could escape, leaving everyone else to die?"

"Something like that."

Humans truly could be as bad as vampires, I thought, then finished climbing the ladder. The closed hatch had a long metal handle. I grabbed it and pulled it toward me, and was able to push the hatch open. No locks after all. I supposed they were more worried about people getting in, than getting out.

I peeked my head up, glancing around. We were in the back of someone's garden.

The night was utterly silent, and my sword issued no warning, so I climbed the rest of the way out of the hatch. I crouched in the shadows of a meticulously trimmed shrubbery while I waited for the men to ascend.

Asher came up next, and stood next to me.

I looked up at him.

He shrugged. "There is no one here to see us. I would hear them breathing."

Feeling a little foolish, I stood as Steifan climbed out of the hatch, then shut it gently behind him, sealing the light of the lantern within.

"Your duke's estate is that way." Asher pointed. "Three gardens down."

I glanced around at the surrounding shrubs, having an odd feeling of noticing them before. I took a few steps toward the fence separating the garden from the street, then froze. I recalled dark hair framing blue eyes, watching me from just this spot.

"This is where I saw Egar," I breathed. I turned back to the men. "The Nattmara knows about the canals." I thought about it. "If he *did* kill Charlotte, he could have moved her body. Maybe he noticed the vampire bite on her neck, and thought it might be a way to lure hunters to the city. The female Nattmara told me our blood has more power than other mortals."

"But why kill Jeramy?" Steifan asked.

My elation abated. Perhaps I was just grasping at threads. "I don't know, I suppose that doesn't really make sense. Why kill Jeramy, and not feed?"

Asher watched us, silently absorbing our words. Or maybe he was just waiting for us to shut up and get on with things, who knew?

"Let's find Vannier," I decided. "Maybe he can answer these questions."

As we started walking, I wondered how I planned to pull the servant out of his bed. I most certainly did not want to be caught breaking into the duke's estate in the middle of the night. At the very least, we would be thrown out of the city. At the most, we would be imprisoned indefinitely, or killed by guards.

We cut across the gardens, scaling fences where necessary, until we reached the duke's estate. I leaned against a tree with Steifan on the other side, both of us hiding in its shadows. Asher stood close behind me, and I couldn't exactly tell him to back up because it would put him out in the open.

Trying to ignore him, I focused my full attention on the back side of the estate. Usually servants' quarters were either in the back, or in a separate building. Since I didn't see any separate buildings, I imagined Vannier's chamber was behind one of the three windows on the bottom floor.

"Wait here," I whispered to Steifan. I didn't bother saying anything to Asher. He would do as he liked regardless, and I wasn't worried about him getting caught.

With my next step in mind, I crept forward, skirting around a garrish white fountain with two scantily clad maidens pouring water from pitchers. I barely breathed as I reached the first of the windows and peeked inside. I could see a bed and small nightstand through gauzy white curtains, but the room appeared to be unoccupied.

I sensed Asher behind me and briefly glanced back at him, then crept to the next window. There was a blanket covered lump on the bed. I couldn't be sure that it was Vannier, but I was pretty sure I could see a tuft of gray hair poking out near the pillow.

I looked back at Asher now peering over my shoulder. *Is that who you saw*, I mouthed, though we would be judging solely on the hair.

Perhaps, he mouthed back.

I nodded, then turned back to the window. Now to get him out of there so we could question him privately.

A tap on my shoulder almost made me scream, but it was only Asher. I was just surprised because he so rarely touched me. He would stand close, yes, but there was always a hair's breadth between us.

He gestured to the sleeping man, then gestured to himself.

Was he offering to fetch Vannier for me? I supposed

that would solve a few problems. *Don't hurt him,* I mouthed.

Asher rolled his eyes, then shooed me away.

I retreated to wait with Steifan back by the tree.

I watched as the shadow of a shape that was Asher disappeared around the side of the house. Not but a few moments later, a stifled shout emanated from within.

I leaned forward, peering around the tree at Steifan.

He shrugged. No more sounds came from within the house.

"There," Steifan whispered.

I followed the direction of his outstretched finger, spotting Asher returning the way he'd come. He clutched Vannier in front of him, one hand covering the old man's mouth while making him walk forward. Vannier wore an old-fashioned sleeping gown, a style now uncommon amongst younger folk.

I caught the wide-eyed look of fear on his face as Asher forced him near, then recognition dawned, and that fear turned to confusion.

Asher maintained his grip over Vannier's mouth, but I suspected the old man wouldn't scream if he let him go. Not without first finding out why two hunters had him pulled from his bed in the middle of the night. We were supposed to be on his side, after all.

I stepped around the tree, facing Vannier. "Earlier tonight," I whispered, "y3ou paid a scarred man. What was his task?"

Vannier's eyes shifted from side to side. He mumbled words, but they were muffled by Asher's hand.

My eyes lifted to Asher. "Let him go. If he shouts, break his neck." I hoped my raised brows conveyed that I didn't actually want him to break the poor man's neck. I didn't think Asher would kill on my command regardless.

He freed Vannier, then took a step back to stand beside Steifan.

I glanced around the dark garden, wishing we had somewhere better to question Vannier, but this would have to do. "Answer the question," I ordered.

Vannier wiped his mouth, then cast a quick glare at Asher before turning back to me. "The man you saw is an old friend. I needed someone I could trust."

I was sure my disbelief showed clearly. "A duke's servant, friends with a mercenary?"

Vannier narrowed his eyes. "I was not always a duke's servant."

Now that, I actually believed. He had wiped away his fear quickly. "And what did you pay this *friend* to do?"

He glanced at the men, then back to me. "I suppose if I must trust someone, it might as well be hunters with few connections in this city."

I didn't correct him in thinking Asher was another Hunter. Better than him realizing what he really was.

Vannier eyed each of us before speaking. "The boy, Bastien, is missing. The duke did not seem surprised by this revelation, so I can only assume he is involved. I contacted an old friend to find out what happened to the boy."

I crossed my arms casually, belying the sudden tension radiating through my body. Bastien was missing. Could he have been taken when I sent him running after our encounter with the mercenaries? "Bastien seemed to think you held little regard for him."

Vannier's wrinkles deepened with a sour expression. "The boy is my grandson. His mother was a drunk, I was forced to disown her early on. When I learned she had perished, I secured a life for the boy."

He couldn't have shocked me more if he admitted to being the duchess' murderer. When I could find the words, I asked, "Bastien doesn't know?"

"What good is a grandfather who abandons his kin? I deserve no relationship with the boy, but I can at least make sure he is all right."

I met Steifan's waiting gaze, knowing we were both thinking the same thing. He had been apprehended, and maybe killed, because of us.

I turned back to Vannier. "Tell us everything you know about the duke and duchess, and about why anyone might not want the duchess' murder solved. I will do everything within my power to find Bastien."

Vannier licked his thin lips, considering my offer. He wrung his wizened hands. "All right, I'll tell you everything, but not here. This information could get me killed. You know of the canals leading out into the city?"

I nodded.

"Good. Meet me at the entrance behind the guild hall at first light. I'll tell you everything, but for now, I must not be found missing."

"We will see you at dawn," I said, gesturing for him to retreat.

Sparing a final glance for us all, he hurried back toward the estate.

Steifan moved to my side as we watched him go. "Do you think we can trust him?"

I sucked my teeth. Bastien was missing, and the duke knew about it. "We're going to have to. Now let's get out of here."

We retreated back through the canals the way we'd come. We would seek out a place to rest, perhaps back near the old keep, then we would meet Vannier at first light. I didn't ask Asher where he was staying, or if we would see him tomorrow night. Despite how much he had helped us, I really didn't want to know.

Chapter Eleven

Vannier awaited us behind the guild hall at first light as promised. Even hidden near the cellar doors, he stuck out like a red flycatcher standing stiff-backed in his showy livery.

His shoulders relaxed as he spotted us coming toward him. "It's about time. I must get back before I'm missed."

I glanced up at the first hint of sunlight just now showing over the rooftops. We were precisely on time, but I didn't bother pointing that out. He didn't have to meet us. I could be patient with a bit of bluster . . . but only a bit.

"Stand guard," I said to Steifan. "I don't want anyone sneaking up on us."

I tugged the hood of my brown traveling cloak forward a little further, making sure it covered all of my hair. Steifan wore a similar cloak. After one attempt on our lives, we couldn't be too careful. I had belted my sword around my waist instead of across my shoulders to make it less conspicuous. The blade was a bit too long for comfort, and it might take me a few moments longer to draw it, but a woman with a greatsword would stand out. At least around my waist, someone searching for me wouldn't spot it from a distance.

Steifan walked out to the narrow intersection and disappeared around the corner. We both had Ryllae's ointment smeared across our eyelids and over our ears, so hopefully even if someone with glamour came, Steifan would be all right.

I turned my attention to Vannier. "Tell me everything you know."

His eyes couldn't seem to settle on a particular part of my face. He wrung his hands, finally meeting my gaze. "You swear to me you will find the boy?"

"I will not give up until he has been found one way or another."

Vannier rubbed his tired eyes. It looked like he hadn't gone back to sleep after we left him. "Lady Charlotte had many secrets, and I was sworn to keep them, but if telling you will help solve her murder and bring back the boy, I will break my oath."

I anxiously waited for him to continue.

He let out a long breath. "Lady Charlotte had a . . . business. She had suitors other than her husband." His lined face grew redder as he spoke.

"If you are trying to tell me she was selling her womanly charms for coin, you can save your breath. Lady Montrant already hinted at as much."

His eyes flew wide for a moment, then he seemed to settle himself. "I suppose that makes this explanation a little easier. Lady Charlotte kept to a regular schedule, and while her business was less than proper, it seemed she was staying safe. Then I noticed the first vampire bite. I caught just a glimpse of it when her sleeve pulled up too far, revealing her wrist."

I lifted my brows. "So the bite on her neck wasn't the first one. How long was this going on?"

"It started a few weeks before she went missing," he explained. "At least that is when I first noticed it happening. It was confusing, to say the least. I had believed that vampires could not feed without killing their victims."

It was a common misconception. "The old ones have more control," I explained. "An older vampire could feed from her roughly once a week without weakening her . . . " I trailed off at a sudden thought, realizing this was the first time anyone actually admitted she had gone missing before she was killed. "Vannier, how long was she actually missing before her body was found, and why did no one report it?"

He'd nodded along to my explanation, though I didn't think he was really listening until I asked the question. His eyes searched my face before he answered, "She was missing for eight or nine days before her body suddenly just showed up in her bed."

"Why didn't the duke tell us she had been missing? Why wouldn't he report it the first night she didn't come home?"

Vannier shook his head. "I don't know, and he made me swear up-and-down that I would not tell you about her business."

If I hadn't suspected the duke before, I most certainly did now. "So he knew about her business? What about the bites?"

He glanced around warily, though there was no one near us. "I cannot say for sure, but he had to know. I wasn't the only one who noticed them. When Lady Montrant noticed, she stopped speaking with Charlotte entirely."

So Lady Montrant knew. She had mentioned the business, and the lack of coin, so why not the bites? "What can you tell me about the Montrants?"

His eyes narrowed and went distant as he seemed to really consider his answer. "They came into a lot of coin this year, but I know little of the circumstances. They are well respected. Lady Montrant was previously one of Charlotte's best friends." He hung his head for a moment. "I fear that is all I can think to tell you. I hope it will be useful."

"You gave us a place to start, at least. We will not leave this city until we figure out what's going on."

He nodded, but I had the feeling once again he wasn't listening to me. If I had to guess, I would say he was genuinely distraught over Charlotte's murder and Bastien's disappearance. He met my gaze, giving me the full force of his gaunt face and the purple marks beneath his eyes. "I would appreciate it if I could leave first. I'd rather avoid being seen with you."

"My, aren't you a charmer."

He didn't seem to get the joke. With a final nod, he hurried past me, then down the adjoining street.

Steifan peeked around the corner. "Learn anything new?"

"A bit. How would you like to take another trip underground?"

He stepped fully around the corner and walked toward me, flapping the hem of his cloak behind him. "I wouldn't like that at all, but I imagine I don't have a choice."

"Well at least you're realistic." I moved toward the cellar doors.

The chain and broken padlock were still on the ground, and one handle barely hung onto the door. If anyone had been here since we had ventured through, they had made no effort to re-seal the entrance.

I hoped it meant no one had been here at all, and we wouldn't be confronted with a knife in the dark, or something far worse.

"Isn't this it?" Steifan questioned, extending the lantern we'd left the previous night toward the ladder.

I peered down the corridor going in the other direction. We could go up to the White Quarter the same way we went before, but it would be difficult to spy from the sunny gardens. "Shine the light down this way. I'm wondering if there are other ways up."

Steifan squeezed past me, heading slowly down the corridor. I could see why someone would need to float Charlotte's body. It would be difficult to carry with how narrow the walkways were on either side of the water.

I considered the layout of the estates above as we walked, wishing I had spent more time in the area. I could roughly judge where we were, but I wasn't sure where we would come up, and we would be doing it in broad daylight.

We stopped as the corridor forked off in two directions, with a metal grate leading over the water to our right.

I glanced one way, then the other. "Would you say we are somewhere near the square where I questioned the illustrious Lady Montrant?"

"I believe we are almost directly beneath it," Steifan answered.

I turned to him, surprised at the surety in his tone.

He shrugged, bobbing the lantern in one hand. "I'm good with directions and distances."

"All right, cartographer, which direction do we go to put us near the Montrant estate?"

He smirked. "While I do not appreciate your sarcasm, I believe we should go left. If there is an exit within the next forty paces, it should lead to the Montrant's garden."

"Remind me to bring you if I ever go spelunking." I gestured for him to walk ahead with the lantern.

We got lucky, finding another ladder up not forty-five paces away.

Steifan held the lantern while I went up first, pausing with my ear near the hatch. I didn't hear anything above, so I turned the handle and opened the hatch a crack. I had expected daylight, but I couldn't see a thing.

"Lantern," I whispered, extending one hand down toward Steifan.

The handle pressed into my palm, and I wrapped my fingers around it, lifting it slowly. When I had enough light to see by, I opened the hatch just a touch more and peered through the crack.

I looked down the length of a wooden floor stretching out into the darkness. The space was still and musty. I was quite sure we'd found our way into someone's cellar. If we were lucky, it was the Montrant's.

I listened for any footsteps or voices, but the rooms above were silent. I opened the hatch the rest of the way and climbed into the cellar, shining the lantern around the space. Along one wall were several barrels next to shelves lined with cheeses, ceramic crockeries, and baskets of goods.

I turned a slow circle as Steifan poked his head up

into the room. The lantern cast odd shadows across metal grating.

My mouth went dry. "Something tells me those cages aren't used to hold dogs."

Steifan climbed into the room, and we both stared at the empty cages lining the far wall. Dirty, tattered rags were scattered within the enclosures, some stained dark reddish brown with dried blood.

"Do you think—" Steifan choked on his own words, lifting a hand to cover his mouth.

I could smell it too. Blood, excrement, and fear. "The missing people. I think they might have been held here, maybe transported through the canals."

His hand still clasped over his mouth, Steifan shook his head. "But for what purpose?" he muttered against his fingers.

I walked closer to the cages, not sure what I hoped to find. "People are stolen away for all sorts of reasons. Judging by the cages, their captors wanted them kept alive." I glanced at the low ceiling above us. "We need to find out where we are. If this is the Montrant's estate, it may help us piece together what happened to Charlotte."

Footsteps echoed across the floor above us, drawing near.

"Down!" I hissed. "Go back down!"

Steifan hopped back through the hatch, barely managing to catch a ladder rung to slow his fall.

My descent was no more graceful, and I nearly lost the lantern on my way down. I had just eased the hatch shut when footsteps hurried down the cellar stairs. I descended the last few steps of the ladder, then waited shoulder to shoulder with Steifan at the bottom.

"Get her in the cage," a man's voice strained.

Muffled cries, then the sound of a cage door slamming shut.

One moment Steifan was standing beside me, and the next he was lunging for the ladder.

I grabbed his shoulder and yanked him back, giving him a demonstration of my unnatural strength. He stumbled, and would have fallen into the water if I hadn't maintained my grip on his cloak.

I jerked his collar, bringing him to face me, then lifted a finger in front of my lips. While his outrage was admirable, we weren't going to stupidly rush into things. The girl was in a cage now, she wasn't going anywhere without us noticing. And if we could follow her, we might find the other missing people, including Bastien.

Steifan's eyes finally focused on me. His jaw was tight, but he nodded.

We both went still as two sets of footsteps echoed up the stairs, leaving behind only the sound of soft crying.

Steifan met my gaze solidly. "We have to get her out of there," he hissed.

I gripped his wrist, just in case. "If we leave her long enough to be transported, we may find the other missing people."

His eyes flew wide. "We can't leave her in a cage, she must be terrified."

I kept my voice low. "Think, Steifan. Her being scared now could save many lives. If the missing people are still in the city, we have to find them. We have to find Bastien."

His expression fell. "We at least have to tell her that we intend to save her."

This was one of those moments where working with someone so new to hunting was a massive detriment. Being a hunter required practicality above all else. We couldn't let one girl's fear risk an unknown number of lives. "If we go up there, she might start screaming, and the missing people could all end up dead. Do you want their blood on your hands?"

It was the first time Steifan had ever looked at me with hatred. My gut clenched, but I knew I was right. He had to see reason, whether he liked that reason or not.

"We will wait right here until she is moved," he said slowly. "We will ensure she comes to no harm."

"Agreed."

He relaxed his stance, probably thinking he had won the battle. In truth, I had planned on waiting here until the girl was moved regardless. I wasn't about to let her slip through our fingers.

I didn't know if this was all related to Charlotte's murder, but it would be a pretty big coincidence if it wasn't. If Charlotte and the duke knew people were being taken, it could've been the reason Charlotte was killed. I needed to figure out who else was involved, and not just to solve a murder. Anyone involved in stealing people away needed to be brought to justice.

My sword felt heavy at my hip, longing to protect the weak from these monsters. For although a sword was perhaps the most brutal form of justice, it was my favorite kind.

Chapter Twelve

I could sense the sky growing dark outside as we waited down in the canal. Eventually the girl above had stopped crying. I genuinely hoped she had fallen asleep to spare herself from waiting in fear.

Steifan sat with his back against the damp stone wall, his shoulders hunched and knees pulled up to his chest. The lantern sat on the ground beside him, the wick pulled low to dampen the flame and preserve oil.

I waited on the other side of the ladder, leaning one shoulder against the stones. I had moved my sword from my hip to my back. If we were to fight, I didn't want to waste the few extra seconds it would take to draw it from my hip.

Steifan looked up toward the ladder at the sound of footsteps. The girl started crying again, her sobs accompanied by the metal creak of the cage door opening.

Steifan stood, and we both waited, looking up at the

ladder. We locked eyes as the footsteps and the sound of crying stopped right above us. Steifan grabbed the lantern, and we both fled around the corner in the direction we'd come.

I peeked around the corner as the hatch door opened, letting a pool of light down into the canal.

"Climb," a man's voice ordered, the same one who had ordered the girl put in the cage.

I saw the hem of a dark colored dress billowing around two small feet coming down the ladder. She wasn't a child, but she most certainly wasn't an adult either. It was difficult to judge for sure in the low lighting.

I pulled myself back around the corner. If they came this way, we would have to run, but I didn't think they would. They weren't bringing this girl to another hatch among the estates, and I doubted they were bringing her to the guild hall, which meant they were going in the other direction we were yet to explore.

By the sounds of it two more people came down behind the girl, but I didn't dare look in case any of them were peering my way. I held the lantern at my other side, shielding the small light with my cloak.

My shoulders relaxed as footsteps headed off in the other direction. I held one arm out, preventing Steifan from trying to follow too closely. They weren't going anywhere in these canals that would prevent us from following at a safe distance.

Once the footsteps had almost faded entirely, I crept

forward, peering around the corner before venturing that way. The straightaway ahead was empty, so I held the lantern out in front of us to keep from falling in the water. It would be a shame if one of us splashing around undid all of our patient waiting.

Steifan followed behind me. Though his steps were light for a normal mortal, they seemed deafeningly loud to my ears. I could only hope the girl and her captors would not expect anyone following them, and so would not be listening for sounds of pursuit.

We reached another fork in the canal, and I peeked out, glancing both ways. Both directions were empty, but I had heard footsteps going across the metal grate to our right, so that was the way I chose.

As we reached the end of the next corridor, I noticed the soft glow of firelight. I handed Steifan the lantern, gesturing for him to stay back. A few more steps and I could tell where the light was coming from. There was a small room built off the side of the canal, probably originally for maintenance supplies, but the girl and her captors were in there now, and it didn't seem they planned on leaving any time soon.

The two men conversed casually, nothing about their current task, while the girl wept.

I crept back to Steifan, debating what to do next. Did we confront the men and hope we could beat enough information out of them to find the other victims? Or did we wait to see who was coming to meet them, because I saw no other reason for them to be dallying.

I quickly decided on the latter and gestured for Steifan to go back around the nearest corner. There, we waited, hoping whoever else was coming would not be venturing from this direction.

Before long we heard a fourth voice, though I hadn't noticed any footsteps.

I peered around the corner. I didn't dare go close enough to look inside the room, but the smell let me know who had arrived. I smelled rich, turned earth, and a prickling sensation danced up and down my skin. The new addition was a vampire. That's why we hadn't heard any footsteps.

If he was here for the girl, we could wait no longer.

I nodded to Steifan in the near darkness, then drew my blade and started forward, leaving our lantern where I had set it. It would be out of oil soon regardless.

I listened for my sword's warning as I tiptoed toward the doorway, but none came. They hadn't noticed us yet, so they didn't mean us harm.

That would soon change.

I stepped into the open doorway, not bothering to sneak in as the vampire would hear me coming long before he spotted me.

He was the first one to turn toward me. He must have only been sixteen when he died, but he was so old his presence felt heavy in my mind. These stupid men were working with an ancient, one who had amassed much coin judging by his fine brocade tunic and velvet pants. Black boots encased his legs up to his knees.

Beyond him were two men I didn't recognize, but judging by their soft bellies and oiled beards, they were middle-aged nobility. They were both near the girl's new cage, one on either side, about to open it.

She trembled in the corner, her face obscured by long, strawberry-blonde hair.

I held my sword at the ready. "You may as well finish opening that cage. I'll be taking her with me."

The vampire's dark eyes seemed to sparkle with amusement, or maybe it was just the torchlight. He flicked a strand of chin length brown hair away from his soft-featured face. "Where is your master, girl? Why has he let you so far off your leash?"

"I needed enough length in my cord to use it to strangle you," I snarled. I stepped further into the room. "Take care of the men," I said to Steifan. "The monster is mine."

"So bold," the vampire said as Steifan moved past my back with his sword drawn. Neither of the men had visible weapons, so he should be fine.

"Where are the other missing people?" I asked the vampire.

The vampire splayed his hands. "I do not require the death of my food. If you cannot find them, it has nothing to do with me."

I edged closer. If I could catch him off guard, I might be able to remove his head before he could attack. If Markus was capable of slaying ancients, then so was I. "You're paying these men to bring you victims so you can live unnoticed within the city. I can hardly believe you would let them go."

"Some I keep, some become my servants, but others have disappeared. If you could help me find them, I'd be most grateful." He smiled at his own jest. He obviously hadn't realized that Steifan and I were both hunters, and I would use that to my advantage.

I stepped closer. The men behind me were muttering to Steifan that none of this was their fault. That they were just doing the vampire's will so he wouldn't kill them.

"Too many have gone missing for just your needs," I said to the vampire. "How many others are involved?"

"That is a question you should ask our friends." He lifted one hand toward the men behind me. "It is none of *my* concern."

So it wasn't just him involved, and it probably wasn't just these two men. I could kill them all, and the operation might continue.

I tightened my grip on my sword. At least it would be a start.

I launched myself at the vampire, swinging my sword through the air. He evaded me, just barely, and my sword came to life, singing through my mind.

The vampire grabbed for me, and I whirled away, slashing at his belly as I went, but missing again.

"You do not fight like a mercenary," he said, dodging another strike.

Our movements had put me in the corner, with the

vampire's back to Steifan and the two men. Steifan had his sword aimed one-handed at the men while he tried to open the girl's cage with the other.

The vampire grabbed for me again, regaining my full attention. "You don't fight like a soldier either. You are something else."

I slashed at him again. He now knew my skills, I may as well tell him. "I am a hunter of the Helius Order, and I have come here for your head."

My hood fell back as I evaded his next lunge. My braid whipped out, following my movements.

"Such red hair," he said, taking a step back. "I have heard of a red-haired hunter being servant to another of my status. To what master do you belong?"

I slashed toward his belly again, and he hopped back. It was more difficult to get close when he wasn't attacking me. All he had to do was stay out of reach. "What does it matter?" I growled.

He took another step back, placing himself near the doorway. "I would not kill the servant of another ancient, lest I bring the rest down upon me. I know our laws."

Curse it all, he was about to run. The Seeing Sword echoed through my mind, urging me to throw it. I obeyed before I could even register the vampire's movements. If I was wrong, and he still intended to attack, he could easily end me.

My sword sailed true, landing with a meaty thunk in the middle of his back. He *had* been turning to run. It was a good thing. I hated to be wrong.

Not sparing a glance for Steifan and the others, I hurried toward the vampire, withdrew my sword, and took his head.

Blood splattered across my cheeks. I lifted my sword, then turned toward the men. Steifan had managed to get the cage open, but the girl was still in it. She appeared to have fainted.

I took a slow step toward the men, depending on my bloody sword and splattered clothing to scare them. Scared men would tell a multitude of secrets.

"Who are you working for?" I asked. "How many others are there?"

Both men lifted their hands, pressing their backs against the wall. "It wasn't our fault. The vampire bespelled us. We had to do what he wanted."

I neared the men, then extended my bloody sword, poking at the fat coin pouch on one man's belt. "If he bespelled you. Why did he feel the need to pay you?"

The man's eyes bulged.

I shifted my sword beneath his belt, pointing the tip at his groin. "If I were you, I would not lie again."

He gasped, plastering himself against the wall. "Please, I'll tell you everything. I'm not the man in charge. I'll give you the man in charge."

I smiled. "Now that's more like it."

I lowered my sword a fraction, then my smile faded. I sensed something else down here, something near. My thoughts went muddy and I nearly dropped my sword as the glamour closed in around my mind like an iron trap.

Chapter Thirteen

I pushed against the magic cloud in my mind, maintaining my tenuous grasp on reality. Steifan's blank expression let me know Ryllae's ointment wasn't strong enough to withstand Egar's magic. The two men we had been questioning stared off at nothing, and the girl was still unconscious. I was on my own.

I sensed Egar as he entered the room. I chanted the ancient words Ryllae had taught me in my head, and visualized myself pulling free of Egar's glamour. I was able to take two steps, turning around to face him, but that was it.

He lifted his blue eyes from the vampire's corpse to observe me. "I see you have learned a new trick. Does this mean you have located the one I hunt?"

The force of his magic lessened, allowing me to speak. "Even if I had, I would not give you what you want. How did you find me down here?"

The corner of his mouth ticked up. "These canals begin in the highlands, bringing water down throughout the entire city. I kept sensing fresh blood beneath my feet, and eventually I found an entrance. It is so easy to find a meal when your prey is already locked up in a cage."

I remembered the ancient saying some of his victims had disappeared. "This was your clue on how to solve my murder. This was what you refused to tell me. How long have you been stealing the vampire's victims?"

He shrugged, stepping around the vampire's corpse to approach me. "Not long. Weak mortals are not my preferred prey, but the vampires will eat anything."

I thought he would come to stand before me, but instead he stepped around me. I was able to shuffle my feet enough to follow him with my eyes. He stood before one of the men, looking him up and down.

Faster than I could follow, he shoved his hand through the man's chest, then ripped out his still-beating heart, cradling it in fingers turned to claws. The man slumped to the ground, dead. He never even screamed.

My heart pounded in my head as I willed myself to move. I chanted Ryllae's words and imagined myself drawing my sword. At the thought of my sword, I finally sensed its presence.

Egar tossed the heart onto the ground, then stepped toward the second man.

"No!" I gasped, but I still couldn't move.

Cast away your fear, a voice said in my mind.

At first I thought I had imagined it, but then it spoke again. *Your fear feeds the creature's magic. Cast it aside.*

I closed my eyes, trying to push away my fear, then a wet sound hit my ears. I opened my eyes to find Egar had killed the second man the same way as the first. He stepped toward Steifan, watching me with a cruel smile. "I think you will tell me what I want to know now." He extended one clawed, bloody hand toward Steifan's chest.

I chanted Ryllae's words over and over again in my head, but beneath them were my own words, or maybe they came from the Seeing Sword. *I am not afraid.*

The words melded in my mind, the ancient words giving strength to the new, which were no less powerful.

Slowly, I reached one trembling hand to my sword. The moment my fingers closed around the hilt, it gave me strength. I drew it, facing the Nattmara. "Touch him and you die."

Egar laughed, stepping away from Steifan. "Do you truly believe you have the strength of will to best me? I have proven time and again that I can crush your mind with a single thought."

My confidence wavered, and fear came crashing through. My grip loosened on my sword hilt.

"I am not afraid," I spoke out loud, echoing my sword's voice in my mind.

My words wiped the grin from Egar's face. "You will bring me to the Sidhe. She cannot hide forever."

So he knew what Ryllae was. I tightened my grip on

my sword and took a step toward him. "She will not have to hide once you are dead."

Egar licked lips thinner than they were just a moment before. His face elongated, making room for rows of pin-sharp teeth. He clicked his long claws together, then charged at me.

My lingering fear fell away as long-honed battle instinct kicked in. All that I knew were his movements and mine. I swung my sword, slashing across his belly.

He reared away with an unearthly shriek, clutching at the deep gash.

I advanced, sword at the ready.

He staggered away from me, his chest heaving, clawed hands gripping at his wound. His words came out warped by long teeth, "Once I find the Sidhe, I will come for you."

He stumbled toward the doorway.

I charged after him, but his glamour hit me like a war horse, making my mind go momentarily black. When I recovered my senses, he was gone.

Trembling, I turned to Steifan.

He blinked a few times, looked down at the two dead men, then back to me. "What in the Light just happened, Lyss?"

I fell to my knees, maintaining my grip on my sword. Without its help, I would have been dead. "The Nattmara. We cannot let him find Ryllae. If he drinks her blood, he will kill us all."

Sensing another presence, I looked back to the

doorway to find Asher standing there. "Took you long enough," I muttered, feeling like I might be sick.

He stepped into the room, taking in the scene. He was the only one of us not covered in blood. Steifan had the worst of it. He'd been standing close to the two men when they were killed.

Asher offered me a hand up. "What happened here?"

I ignored his hand and stood on my own. "We figured out what has been happening to the missing people. They are being sold to vampires for blood. We followed the two men bringing the girl down here, then the Nattmara came."

Asher looked me over, lingering on the blood staining my shirt and cloak. "And the dead vampire? He was here to buy the girl?"

I nodded, then frowned, remembering the vampire's words. "He said he had heard of me, and that he couldn't kill me because I belong to another ancient. He tried to run."

Asher's expression gave nothing away. "He surrendered, and you killed him as he fled."

If he wanted an apology, he wasn't going to get one from me. "He was buying this girl. He would have kept her like a slave."

"I did not ask for justification."

I sighed, feeling like my knees were about to give out. I had just faced the Nattmara, and here we were discussing a vampire's death. "You may not have asked for justification, but you wanted me to know that you disapproved. Well, I know it, and I stand by what I did."

Asher lowered his chin, draping his white hair across his high cheekbones. "I would expect no less from you."

There were one-hundred different ways to interpret his words, so I didn't try. I turned to Steifan as he retrieved his fallen sword and sheathed it. "Can you carry the girl? I want to get out of here before Egar decides to come back."

Steifan nodded, then knelt by the cage, gently pulling the unconscious girl into his arms.

I was ready to go, but Asher was still looking at the two dead men.

"Hungry?" I asked, then instantly regretted it. I had used all of my energy breaking the Nattmara's glamour. I was getting cranky.

"The Nattmara killed them where they stood," he observed, ignoring my foulness. "They did not struggle." He looked to me. "His glamour is this strong, and you managed to break it?"

Suddenly I was uncomfortable. In truth, I was just as surprised as he. "My sword helped," I muttered.

He observed me closely, probably wondering if I was joking, though he knew the sword was sentient. What-ever conclusion he reached, he did not question further. "I found another entrance near the old keep. Perhaps we should go that way."

"Lead on." I gestured toward the doorway with my

bloody sword. For some reason, I didn't feel quite ready to put it away.

I followed behind Asher, and Steifan behind me. We found our lantern with just enough oil to see us out. The girl never woke as we walked, and I hoped she would not until morning. I didn't want her to wake screaming in the night. Better to wake when she could see her surroundings and know that she was safe.

We would take her back to where she belonged, and she would be safe. It was more than I could say for the rest of us.

Chapter Fourteen

The entrance Asher had found let out just south of the old keep. It was another old cellar, like the one behind the guild hall. As we climbed out into the moonlight, I wondered if there was another entrance near where we had found Jeramy's body.

With Steifan still carrying the unconscious girl, we searched for a private area in the keep. We would need to watch her until she woke. Unfortunately, dawn was still well off. I was hungry and cold, more cold than the weather permitted. It was like pushing Egar out of my mind had taken the very warmth from my veins.

Asher found a small alcove, protected on three sides by ruined walls still tall enough to conceal us.

I helped Steifan remove his cloak, then spread it on the ground for him to set the girl upon it. We tugged the edges of the cloak around her, leaving her to rest.

Asher watched us silently.

I glanced at him as I stood. "I appreciate you escorting us out of the canals, but there is no reason for you to stay here any longer."

He didn't move. He just stood there like a tall, brooding statue. "We need to speak about the ancient you killed, and the Nattmara."

Steifan looked back and forth between the two of us. "I think I'll go see if I can find a bit of wood for a fire." He retreated from the alcove, though he probably wanted sleep even worse than I did.

I bundled my cloak around me, suppressing a shiver. My sword had remained silent at my back after it helped me with the Nattmara. "What else is there to talk about?"

Asher stepped close, looming over me. "You are my servant, and you killed an ancient."

I hiked one shoulder in a small half shrug. "Three other ancients were killed the night Karpov died, why is this one any different?"

Ire flickered through his silver eyes, making me suddenly nervous. "Those who had joined Karpov had turned against us. The vampire you killed tonight tried to leave you in peace. He respected our laws."

Anger prickled my skin. "He was trying to *buy* that girl." I gestured to the small, cloak-wrapped bundle behind me. "And he had bought others. If I left him alive, more would have been kidnapped. I can only hope his death will set an example for the other vampires in the city."

Asher lifted his chin. "My kind must feed, Lyssandra, it is what we are. Many are not strong enough to bespell victims and not take too much blood."

I stepped closer, my indignance making me bold. "If vampires kill, I hunt them. That is what *I* am."

"I am well aware, but your self-righteous attitude has furthered Karpov's plan. One ancient was already killed several nights ago. And now another has perished. Soon there will be too few of us to control the young ones."

My back hunched. He was right, I had helped Karpov from beyond the grave. But it could have been no other way. The kidnappings had to stop.

Asher watched me. "Your expression hints that you have seen reason, though experience tells me that cannot be the case."

I rubbed my eyes, slowly shaking my head. "I do see the reason behind your words, but you cannot ask me to forsake my oaths. I am sworn to protect innocents."

"If you're going to help me discover who killed the other ancient, you will need to be amongst more of my kind. I cannot bring you near them if you plan to personally present justice for their crimes."

I tried to call back my anger, but it was no use. I was just too tired. "The dead deserve justice."

"Perhaps, but it does not always have to be dealt by your hand."

I looked up at him. "How about this. If I am to meet a vampire, forewarn them to commit no crimes in front of me. If I do not personally see them attacking or killing someone, I will have no need to hunt them."

A smile tugged at the corner of his lips. "My, what a generous compromise."

I glared, tugging my cloak more tightly around me. "My advice to you would be to accept what you can get."

Steifan peeked back into the alcove to find Asher grinning. He seemed to take it as a sign that it was safe to return, and stepped the rest of the way into the space, a few small jagged pieces of wood bundled under one arm.

He tossed the wood into the dirt. "I was able to beg a flint and steel from a merchant caravan. They didn't seem to want to ask any questions once they noticed the blood on my clothes."

I used the distraction to step away from Asher. "We need to discuss the Nattmara. We must seek out his lair and weaken him before he can find—" I hesitated, not wanting to speak Ryllae's name out loud. "What he seeks," I finished.

Asher followed me to stand in front of the fire Steifan was attempting to build. "It nearly killed you tonight, now you want to find its lair?"

Steifan and Asher both looked at me as I explained, "The Nattmara's lair is its place of power, a site for ritual magic. When I slew Egar's sister, I was able to weaken her by destroying a ritual urn."

"But Egar is as much Sidhe as he is Nattmara," Steifan countered. "His magic may not be the same."

He was right, but I didn't know what else to do. I couldn't just wait around for Egar to find us again. "He travels the canals. If he does have a lair, I think it is somewhere down there. It is the only way I can think of to weaken him."

Smoke billowed up from Steifan's small wood pile. "And what about everything else we discovered tonight?" Steifan asked. "We must remember we are here to solve Duchess Auclair's murder."

I sat in the dirt, extending my cold hands toward the first small flames. "Tomorrow we will go to Duke Auclair and tell him what we know. He can either admit his role in things, or we will take our findings to the Archduke."

"What about the Montrants?"

I stared down into the flames, wondering if the Potentate had known what he was sending us into. "Let us start with the duke. We don't actually have any solid evidence, so having his testimony will help. If he is frightened enough, he may tell us if the Montrants are in charge, or simply just involved."

My shoulders began to relax from the fire's warmth. I longed for my comfortable bed at Castle Helius, with four safe walls and a locked door.

Asher loomed over the fire, but did not sit. I was pretty sure vampires never got cold. "You should rest," he said to me. "I will keep watch."

I gave him an incredulous look. "You expect me to trust you enough to sleep in front of you?"

He stared at me, his face impassive.

I chewed the inside of my cheek. I didn't need a vampire watching over me. I didn't *want* a vampire watching over me. But Steifan and I were alone in this city. The Nattmara was out there, and I couldn't forget that someone had been hired to kill us. So maybe I just didn't *want* a vampire watching over me, but the need would have to outweigh my pride, if only to keep Steifan and the girl safe for the night.

"Fine," I acquiesced.

Steifan gave me a shooing gesture with his hands across the fire, urging me to say more.

I gritted my teeth. "You have my thanks."

Asher shrugged and walked toward the opening of the alcove. "Consider it pre-payment for the aid you will give me once we are back in the mires."

I stared at his back for a moment, then shook my head. Usually, I found men easy to understand, but the vampire perplexed even me.

Steifan had already laid on his back in the dirt and closed his eyes. *He* didn't seem perplexed by the vampire.

I tugged my hood up, then curled on my side near the fire, wrapping my cloak around me. I left my sword on, just in case. Maybe I didn't understand men as well as I thought, though I really hated being wrong.

I closed my eyes, willing myself to rest. While I could have gone another night or two without sleep, there was no saying what morning might bring, and I needed to restore my energy if I was to hunt the Nattmara.

As I fell in and out of wakefulness, I sensed Asher's eyes on me from time to time, and I noticed when he added a bit more wood to the fire.

Eventually I forced myself to actually sleep. After all, he could only watch us until dawn. For as human as he sometimes seemed, he was still a creature of the night. And that was a fact I would never forget.

MORNING CAME TOO SOON, AND MY STOMACH WAS painfully empty. I sat up to find Steifan already awake, speaking with the girl, who seemed calm.

"Why didn't you wake me?" I groaned.

Steifan and the girl both looked to me. She seemed older now than I had originally thought, just small-boned.

"Asher woke me when he had to leave," Steifan explained. "He said you expended too much energy last night . . . *dealing* with things. He asked that I let you rest."

I pinched my brow as a dull ache started between my eyes. "I would like to argue, but I cannot. I don't usually sleep so deeply."

"Perhaps he knows what's best for you." Steifan winked.

I rubbed my sore head as the ache progressed. "I

really wish I had something to throw at you right now." I turned my attention to the girl. "Are you alright?"

She nodded, though her eyes were a touch wary.

"She lives not far from here," Steifan explained. "She didn't know the man who took her from the square, nor did she at any time see anyone she recognized."

Though I felt like a sack of manure, I forced myself to stand. "We will walk you home then," I said to the girl. "I would ask that you hide away for the next few days until we make sure we find everyone involved in kidnapping you."

As she stood, I looked her up and down, ending with her bare feet. "What happened to your shoes?" I asked.

"They took them when I tried to run away. They said if I tried again, they would cut off my feet. Steifan says you don't yet know who took me."

I sighed. "We have a few ideas. Are you acquainted with any of the nobility?"

Frowning, she shook her head.

I believed her. She had probably just been randomly chosen. Like the Nattmara said, vampires will eat just about anything.

I tugged up my hood, covering my hair, then moved the Seeing Sword back to my belt. "Let's go, I need something to eat."

I turned away, heading out of the alcove. Steifan and the girl followed. It was an effort to keep my dizziness at bay. I hadn't realized how much I had pushed myself to break the Nattmara's glamour.

While I was reluctant to visit Ryllae again, I might just have to find her after we visited the duke. I needed to be better prepared to break Egar's glamour, or else next time I faced him—with him ready for my new skills—I would lose.

Chapter Fifteen

Mid-morning found us back at the wrought iron gates leading to the wealthy district, arguing with the two guards, *again*. At least the girl's husband had insisted he provide us with a meal when we brought her home, else I would not have been able to maintain my temper.

I was barely maintaining it as it was.

The guard arguing fervently with us was the same one who had escorted us to the duke's estate. "Come back in proper attire, and I will let you through," he said for the hundredth time.

Steifan and I were both still in our traveling cloaks. The fabric was dark enough to hide the blood stains, and we used them to cover the more obvious stains on our clothing underneath.

I crossed my arms. "We are not leaving to simply change into our armor and return. Just the other day you didn't want us passing with armor and weapons. Now you want us to have them?"

He glanced at the sword still obvious at my hip, even though it was mostly covered by my cloak. "You still have weapons, and now you don't even look like hunters of the Helius Order. I won't be up on charges of letting mercenaries past my guard."

"But we're *not* mercenaries," I growled.

"But you *look* like mercenaries."

I wanted to argue that we could just go through the bloody canals and bypass them, but one, I didn't want him to know we knew about them, and two, I didn't want to risk running into Egar again before we could confront the duke.

Steifan and I both turned at footsteps approaching our backs. It was the duke himself, looking disheveled and flustered. Surprisingly, he seemed relieved to see us. "I've been looking for you two everywhere. Come with me." His beady eyes scorned the guards yet blocking our way. "What are you waiting for? Open the gate."

The guards hurried to obey, and I couldn't help my smug smile as Steifan and I followed the duke through the entrance.

Not saying a word, the duke led the way toward his estate.

I glanced at Steifan as we followed the duke's podgy, brocade-clad form, my brows lifted in question.

Steifan shrugged. So we both didn't know why the

duke had sought us out personally, rather than sending Vannier or another servant.

We reached the estate, then waited while the duke ascended the short exterior stairs, opening the door himself. No sign of Vannier within. We went inside, and the duke shut and locked the door behind us.

"Upstairs," he said. "I don't want to risk someone listening at any of the windows."

We followed him across the sitting room, then up the stairs. The situation was getting stranger and stranger, but my sword hadn't warned me. We weren't being lured into a trap.

Once we were upstairs, the duke gestured for us to go through the first doorway, which led into a large office. Open shutters let in a cool breeze. There were two chairs on the far side of the desk, opposite the over-cushioned monstrosity meant for the duke.

I decided against either chair, opting to lean my back lightly against the wall just inside the doorway.

The duke didn't seem to take offense. He hurried around Steifan, then stood facing us both. He tugged a handkerchief from his vest pocket, wiping the sheen of sweat from his forehead. "I have something I must admit to both of you. My life is in danger."

I crossed my arms, waiting for him to continue. If he was about to tell us everything, there was no need to threaten him yet with the information we had discovered.

He glanced around the office, as if someone else had

followed us up the stairs, but we were entirely alone. I heard nary a sound from the rest of the house.

"I didn't find Charlotte's body here," he breathed. "I found her rotting in the slums."

He seemed to expect surprise from us, but neither of our faces gave anything away. I nodded for him to continue.

He licked his lips, considering his next words. "I knew she wasn't killed by the vampire who bit her, but I needed a reason to bring in outside help. I wanted hunters to investigate her murder because too many of the city guard are involved."

I lifted my brows. He had finally managed to surprise me. "You wanted us to investigate, even though you knew she wasn't killed by a vampire?"

He nodded quickly, his eyes wide. "I can trust no one within the city. I needed outside help. I . . . I wanted out, and they killed her as a warning to me."

I decided to put him out of his misery, if only to speed the conversation along. "You were involved in the kidnappings, and you knew they were being sold to vampires."

He paled. "How did you—"

"You wanted us to investigate, did you not? We could tell Charlotte had been moved here through the canals after her death, and we found Jeramy DeRose. And you obviously know that two men and a vampire were killed in the canals last night, or else you wouldn't have so desperately sought us out this morning."

The duke hung his head, shuffling around the desk to slump down into his chair. He rubbed his eyes with one plump hand. "They think I sent you down into the canals. They've realized why I really called you here."

I stepped toward the desk. "Who are they? Who is in charge?"

"So you haven't figured out everything then," he muttered. "Bellamy Montrant. He is the one who made the deal with the vampires. Charlotte had started a . . . business, else we would have gone destitute. When Bellamy approached me with an opportunity, I jumped at it. I would have done anything so that Charlotte could . . ."

Steifan moved forward and took one of the chairs across the desk from the duke. "We know of Charlotte's business, you can speak freely."

I blinked at them both, realizing something. The duke was a terrible man, but he did have an ounce of honor to him after all. "That's why you didn't want us to have Charlotte's ledger. You didn't want anyone else knowing her secret. You hoped we could solve her murder without uncovering that aspect."

His face pinched and grew red. "So you knew about the ledger, then. I did want to keep her secret buried. She deserved that much consideration, at least. When she started coming home with the vampire bites, I worried she was going to get herself killed. I think—" he shook his head. "I think she was actually in love with the creature, and she never would have met him had I not involved us in Montrant's scheme."

I nodded along. "You tried to pull out to get her away from the vampire, and you think Montrant killed her to send you a message. But why was she meeting with Jeramy DeRose?"

He hung his head. "That was my fault too. I knew Montrant was watching me, so I sent Charlotte there instead. Jeramy was the first person Bellamy approached about his scheme. When he refused, the Montrants ruined him. I thought if we went to Jeramy, we might have enough evidence to approach the Archduke."

"And you think Montrant killed them both," I finished for him. "When Charlotte never returned, you went looking for her body, and knowing she had vampire bites, you devised your plan. But why wait so long to bring her body home? The rot would suggest she was in Jeramy's home for quite some time."

He grimaced. "I had to figure out a way to bring her body back without anyone seeing it, but I didn't know who to trust. I knew she was supposed to meet with the vampire the following week. She always met him on the same night, so I went in her stead. I think the creature loved her too, as much as he was able. He helped me move her body."

I stared at him. "If the vampire really loved her, why didn't he avenge her?"

The duke looked like he was trying to swallow something sharp. "He said there was an ancient vampire involved, and he could not stand against him. After he helped me move Charlotte's body, he fled the city. He agreed that I should contact the Helius Order, but wanted to be nowhere near once you arrived."

"Smart vampire," Steifan muttered.

I considered all the duke had told us. It made sense. If he would repeat the story to the Archduke, and we could provide validity by backing up his claims, we might just get permission to launch a full investigation. No more sneaking through canals or having our way barred by guards.

"We will go to the Archduke immediately," I decided. "You will repeat everything you have told us."

His eyes went wide. He stood, staggering backwards with palms outstretched. "No, you don't understand. I'll be killed before I can utter a word. Too many guards are involved." He backed away until he was near the open window. "You'll have to go to the Archduke yourselves."

I heard the bolt release outside, and opened my mouth to shout a warning, but I was too late. The duke's body lurched forward as an arc of blood erupted from his neck.

Steifan hopped over the desk to land beside the fallen duke while I rushed to the window. I peered out just in time to see a figure in the duke's garden, hiding a crossbow in the folds of his loose cloak. A hood shadowed his face.

I rushed passed Steifan and out into the hall, then took the stairs down two by two. I exited the estate, then practically flew back to the garden, vaulting over the tall fence. I whipped around, scanning the manicured shrubs and the garrish fountain.

I cursed under my breath. I hadn't been fast enough. The garden was empty, and I had seen the duke's wound. He would not survive to tell his tale again.

"Lyss!" A voice I recognized called out.

It was almost too much to hope for, but when I turned I spotted Tholdri's golden hair out on the street beyond the fence. He wore his full armor, with a sword at his shoulder.

I cast a final glance around the garden, then ran toward him. "What in the Light are you doing here?"

He gave me a smug smile and leaned his hands against the fence. "I convinced the Potentate to let me come. I told him I was worried you would get into trouble amongst the nobles. I was just coming to Duke Auclair's to look for you."

I shook my head, overwhelmingly grateful to see him, but too busy to express it. "We need to get back inside. Someone just hit the duke with a crossbow through the window. I ran out here looking for them, but they're gone."

His eyes widened. "Why wasn't that the first thing out of your mouth when you saw me?"

He turned away from the fence, leaving me to vault over it and catch up to his back as he walked toward the door. We both hurried inside and up the stairs, finding Steifan just about to come down them.

His grim expression and bloody hands told me what I already knew. "He's dead." He looked to me. "Did you find who shot the bolt?"

I stepped next to him and shook my head. "I wasn't fast enough, Tholdri found me as I was searching the garden."

Steifan looked to Tholdri. "I must say, I'm glad to see you. We have found ourselves in quite the mess. Has Lyss told you about the Nattmara?"

Tholdri blinked at me. "Now *that's* what you should have started with. The one from Charmant?"

I sighed. "We have much to catch you up on, but first we need to fetch the guards and let them know the duke is dead. If we are lucky, they'll believe we didn't do it."

"Perhaps it was unwise of me to come after all," Tholdri said.

I started down the stairs. "You have no idea."

"Asher is here," I heard Steifan whisper to Tholdri at my back.

Tholdri chuckled. "A fresh murder, an ancient vampire, and a Nattmara. Traveling with Lyss is never dull, is it?"

I reached the foot of the stairs and went for the door. "We will add two more murders to the list if you two don't shut up."

Masculine laughter followed me out the door.

Tholdri was right. My life was a lot of things. Dull was not one of them.

.

Chapter Sixteen

The guards didn't blame us. Imagine that. It was clear that the bolt came from outside, and someone on the street had seen the cloaked man running away and confirmed that it wasn't Tholdri. Though that still left us with knowing everything, but having no evidence or reliable testimony.

We explained everything to Tholdri as we headed back toward the old keep, since I wasn't sure where else to go. I didn't think the duke's death would cancel out the contract on our heads. In fact, it would be safe to assume things had escalated. The duke had been killed for what he had to tell us, and now we knew highly dangerous information.

Tholdri glanced around the ruins of the old keep. Many of the camps had cleared out by the light of day with most of the traveling merchants down at the main square.

"We have to go back to the canals," I decided. "We'll find proof to take to the Archduke." I leaned my back against a crumbling stone wall and looked up at the gray sky. Rain would come by midday.

"What about the Nattmara?" Steifan asked, leaning against the wall beside me.

I shook my head. "I don't know. I'm not sure if I could break his glamour again now that he would be ready for me. I wounded him, but there's no saying how fast he might heal."

"Should we go back to Ryllae?" he asked.

Finished looking around, Tholdri stood in front of us. "Who is Ryllae?"

I winced at the second mention of her name. I doubted Egar was watching us, but just in case, I didn't want to give him any more information on her if I could help it. "She is someone whose name we should not say out loud. She taught me how to break the Nattmara's glamour, but we can't risk returning to her now when her blood could make him practically immortal."

Steifan moved away from the wall to look at me. "If he kills us, there will be nothing to stop him from finding her. I think it might be worth the risk."

"He has a point," Tholdri said, always one to catch on quickly.

"She has strong glamour," Steifan added. "She can protect herself."

I mulled it over. My breathing felt too shallow, on the verge of panic. Could I face Egar again without further preparation? "Fine," I decided, "we will go to her. *I* will go to her. You two will hang back and make sure no one is watching."

Tholdri looked to Steifan. "She has become far more reasonable since she started spending time with you."

"Or far more stupid," I muttered, pushing away from the wall.

Tholdri laughed, and both men turned to follow me.

I kept my eyes trained on my surroundings as I walked, ignoring the presence of Tholdri and Steifan behind me. If I led Egar to Ryllae . . .

I could not think of that now. Steifan and Tholdri were right, I needed the tools to defeat the Nattmara. If I could not kill him, he would find Ryllae eventually, with or without my help.

We reached the small structure Ryllae called home. A few men and women stood around, watching goods and wagons left behind by the merchants gone to market for the day. Steifan lingered near one of the larger camps. Tholdri had diverted. I didn't see him, but I knew he would be watching.

An older woman dressed in bright foreign silks eyed me as I neared Ryllae's doorway. "She's not there. I heard a struggle near dawn."

My breath left my body, and I was frozen for a moment. Then I took an aching inhale and rushed through Ryllae's doorway, taking in the signs one by one. Blood on the hard-packed earth. Ashes from the fire scattered. A few belongings strewn about.

My heart thundered in my ears. No mortal would be able to take one of the Sidhe on their own. Egar had found her.

I rushed back outside, spotting Steifan.

He met me halfway. "What happened?"

I shook my head over and over. This was my fault. I hadn't been able to finish Egar off, and now he had found Ryllae. "He has her. He has Ryllae. We need to search the canals, we have to find his lair."

Steifan's eyes went wide. "But what if his lair isn't in the canals?"

I reached out and gripped his arms. "It has to be."

Tholdri appeared at my side. I turned to explain things to him, but he shook his head. "I heard, let's go."

I nodded. "There is an entrance to the canals not far from here. We'll start with that. If Ryllae is still alive—"

"We will find her," Tholdri cut me off. "I promise."

With another nod, I turned and led the way, not speaking my final thought. *Don't make promises you can't keep.*

WE CREATED A MAKESHIFT TORCH TO LIGHT OUR WAY. Fortunately Steifan still had his borrowed flint, and I still had Ryllae's ointment. We smeared it on our eyes and ears, for what good it would do.

I led us deep into the damp darkness, praying we

could find Ryllae in time. If she was already dead, Egar would kill us all.

We passed the tunnel that would take us to the trap door in the estate cellar. I knew that direction led to other trapdoors among the estates, then eventually to the exit behind the guild hall. I didn't think Egar would be in that direction, else we would have seen signs of him. If he was stealing the vampire's victims, he was probably somewhere close to where they were held, but far enough to not be discovered.

We reached the place where the two men and ancient vampire fell. I held the torch inside, taking a quick glance around. The bodies were gone, the cage empty. I moved on. Steifan and Tholdri followed silently at my back.

Fear made my hand clammy around the torch. Cold sweat dripped down my brow. I could not recall being so frightened since the night Karpov killed my uncle, so many years ago.

We reached another intersection and I had to make a choice, because there was no way we were splitting up. I closed my eyes, reaching out with my senses. I could usually sense vampires when they were near, and I knew the feel of Egar's magic. I had to try.

Steifan and Tholdri didn't speak a word. They trusted me. It was nice to know I had good friends, especially since we all might die before nightfall.

My senses found nothing but darkness. The running

water seemed impossibly loud. I cursed under my breath. I didn't know which way to go.

I was about to take my chances and head left when I felt a prickling at my back. It didn't feel like Egar, it felt like Ryllae. Was she still alive? Had she sensed me and managed to reach out?

"This way," I whispered to the men. "Be prepared."

I turned right, breaking into a run with the torch's flame wavering wildly. I took countless turns, and knew if I managed to survive, I might have trouble finding my way back out. Tholdri and Steifan's footfalls echoed at my heels. Just as my lungs started to burn, I sensed it. Great, concentrated magic. Egar's lair was near.

My sword awoke, sensing the magic too, but I didn't slow. Egar would know I was coming.

I reached another bend and turned with Tholdri and Steifan breathing hard behind me. I turned again, running down a more narrow passage with no water flowing through it. Parts of the walls were crumbled, strewing rubble across my path. If I couldn't sense the magic so strongly, I would have passed the entrance. But I did sense it, so strong it was nearly overwhelming. What had once been a doorway was now half-filled with debris.

I halted so abruptly Tholdri had to reach out his arms, bracing on either side of the narrow tunnel to stop himself from running into me.

I drew my sword in one hand with the torch in the other, then squeezed through the narrow opening, which led into a vacant tunnel with a long-dry canal. This must have been part of the original canal system, long since replaced with newer tunnels. Further down, soft light emanated from a doorway.

I approached cautiously with Steifan and Tholdri following close behind, slowing as I neared the doorway. The smell of blood was so overwhelming for a moment I thought we were too late, but then I realized I could still feel Ryllae's magic urging me forward.

"Greetings hunters," a distorted voice echoed from within the chamber.

I handed the torch back to Steifan, gripped my sword in two hands, then entered the chamber.

My stomach lurched. The floor was coated in blood, both old and new, with body parts strewn about. In the center of the room was Ryllae, lying eerily still on her back.

Egar hunched over her, clutching her small body with long claws. He lifted his face, catching the candlelight in the room to show rows of sharp teeth dripping with Ryllae's blood. I took a step closer to see a wound at her neck.

The Seeing Sword's magic flowed through me, eager to slay the monster before us.

Egar's glistening eyes looked past me. "I see you have brought me a feast."

He meant Steifan and Tholdri, but I didn't dare look back at them. "Step away from her," I ordered. "It is time we end this."

He stood, and if I didn't know any better I'd say he'd grown taller. He used his sleeve to wipe the blood from his malformed mouth. "It is too late. The Sidhe's blood has strengthened me. I will cut off your legs and keep you here to feed from in the future."

His glamour slammed into me. Everything went gray, then I felt a sharp stinging pain at my throat. I staggered back, clutching the hilt of my sword for dear life. I couldn't see, I couldn't hear. I didn't know where Steifan and Tholdri were.

The Seeing Sword came alive, pushing back a small measure of the glamour. I felt blood trickling down my throat, but the wounds caused by Egar's claws seemed shallow. He could have killed me in that first rush, but either his desire to draw things out—or to keep me alive for later—had stopped him.

I still couldn't see, but I could sense Egar's movements. He circled me, and I was able to move my feet to follow his pacing, keeping my sword between us.

Egar stopped moving. "Tricky girl with your strange sword. But can you sense your companions? Are they already dead?"

My hands trembled so violently that I nearly dropped my sword. It urged me to remain calm, but my fear was winning. Why could I sense Egar, but not Steifan and Tholdri? Had he killed them as soon as he blinded me?

A different kind of magic seeped into my consciousness. Ryllae. She was still alive. Her old words coursed through my mind. I had forgotten to use them, but she was using them for me now. The gray began to lift from my vision.

Egar's shriek of rage was the only warning I had. My sword moved, but I didn't remember moving it. It was as if it guided my arms and not the other way around. I felt it slide into Egar's flesh.

He shrieked again, but more importantly, his glamour lessened. I was finally able to see the room. Tholdri still stood in the doorway, staring blankly. Next to him, Stefan blinked, as if trying to focus his eyes on me.

I tore my gaze away from them and advanced on the Nattmara.

He pressed his back into the corner. I could feel his glamour tearing at my mind as he clutched his torn abdomen.

"How?" he rasped. "How are you keeping me out? The Sidhe couldn't even keep me out."

I didn't bother to explain that my sword and Ryllae had helped me. I lunged forward, shoving my blade up through his chest. He grunted, and I pulled it out in a wash of blood. He fell to his knees, but still he did not die.

"How?" he gasped again. "With her blood I should have been immortal."

I raised my sword over my shoulder. "Ask me how many *immortals* I have killed, and maybe it will make sense to you."

I didn't give him time to ask. I swung my sword, parting his head from his shoulders. I watched his head rolling across the floor, and could have sworn it blinked before the eyes finally went distant with death.

Panting, I lowered my sword, glancing back toward Steifan and Tholdri.

Steifan was the first to come to. He looked at me, his eyes registering the death of the Nattmara, then he rushed to Ryllae.

I was at her other side in an instant, placing my bloody sword on the stone floor beside me. I knelt over her, checking her blood-slick neck for a pulse. Her bleeding had slowed, but there was a big pool on the ground and who knew how much had gone down Egar's mouth.

I nearly jumped out of my skin when her eyes fluttered open. She lifted a hand to her throat, her fingers trembling like butterfly wings. "You came." Her words gurgled, letting me know she had blood in her airway, but she seemed to be healing. Even now, I could see her torn skin slowly beginning to reknit.

If she healed faster than a vampire, could Egar do the same? I whipped my gaze back to his body, then managed to calm myself. His head still remained fully parted from his shoulders. But seeing how well Ryllae could heal, I knew I'd be burning his body before I'd be able to sleep at night.

Tholdri had finally regained his senses and came to stand over us. "What in the Light just happened?"

I looked up at him. "Glamour. Steifan seems to have more of a resistance to it than you."

Steifan stayed kneeling at Ryllae's other side. "I could hear what was going on, but I couldn't see nor move." Ryllae reached out for his hand, and he helped her sit up.

She still clutched her throat, but the color was returning to her cheeks.

"How is she healing?" Tholdri asked.

Ryllae looked at me, managing a pained smile. "You really do know how to keep a secret, don't you?"

"That she does," Steifan said.

Tholdri put his hands on his hips, looming over us. "Would someone please tell me what's going on?"

I stood. "The Nattmara is dead, and his victim will survive. Does it matter how she manages to heal?"

"You're infuriating."

With Steifan's help, Ryllae stood. "It is not her secret to tell, just be grateful that she shares her own with you."

I raised a brow at her. "How do you know that?"

She shrugged, then winced. "They are both important to you. When I helped you overcome the glamour, I could sense that your greatest need was to protect them."

Though he still didn't fully know what was going on, Tholdri grinned and put an arm around my shoulder. "That's our Lyss. Just a big softy."

I shoved his arm away with a laugh, glancing once more at the Nattmara. It was hard to believe he was actually dead. I searched for the torch, finding it had rolled against the wall right next to the doorway.

"Let's burn the body here," I said. "I don't want to risk him ever coming back, and we still need to bring justice to Duke and Duchess Auclair before the day is through. Maybe if we approach the Montrants covered in blood, we can scare them into confessing." I meant my words in jest, but thinking about it, maybe it wasn't such a bad idea.

"They are the culprits of your murder investigation?" Ryllae asked.

"Yes," I answered, "and they have been kidnapping people to sell them to vampires. The Nattmara was stealing some of the victims."

"And you would like to scare them into confessing?" she asked.

"I meant it half-joking," I explained. "I don't know how we would scare them enough to confess."

Seeming more steady on her feet, Ryllae smiled. "I believe I can help with that."

I found her smile unsettling, but I wouldn't turn down the help.

Just how frightening could one of the Sidhe be? We were about to find out.

Chapter Seventeen

W e burned the Nattmara where he lay. I filled Ryllae in on the rest of the details of the murders. She had actually met Charlotte before, and believed she could help.

Our first step was to leave a bloody piece of parchment in the Montrant's cellar, and I was quite sure after the duke's confession that it had been their cellar where we had first found the kidnapped girl.

That first step was easy, the next, more difficult. We had decided to wait until nightfall, which would give us time to make ourselves more presentable. Of the three of us, I was the most grotesque, covered in blood both old and new with three scratches already healing at my throat.

Seeing no other option, I bathed in the cold dark water of the canal. I ended up with sopping wet hair and clothing, trudging back toward the canal entrance near the old keep. Once we were above ground, I hung my outer layers of clothing to dry. Ryllae stayed with us, prepared to protect us with her glamour if need be.

Yet there was no need. We waited out the rest of the day, which stretched on impossibly long, and eventually my clothes had dried enough to wear. Now that Egar was dead, my mind was consumed with getting justice for the Auclairs, and for all the missing people. We had never found Bastien or Vannier, so I could only guess that they were dead. Maybe once the Montrants confessed, they could tell us where to find their bodies.

Ryllae stood beside me as I watched the sun making its slow descent. Steifan and Tholdri had gone to buy food and a new lantern, and it was the first time we had been alone since she had first taught me about glamour.

"Your sword is special," she said, tucking a lock of dark hair behind her ear. Her throat was fully healed, though blood still stained her clothing.

I startled. "How do you know?"

"I've been alive a long time. I've seen something like it before. It speaks to you."

"Could you hear it?" I hesitated, surprised at how easily I admitted the secret.

She shook her head. "No, I would need to touch it to hear it, and I would rather not. Such magic can sometimes leave a residue. Where did you find it?"

There were few secrets between us now, so I saw no reason not to tell her. "The Potentate of the Helius Order gave it to me. It woke to my touch."

"I imagine it did," she said. "That blade was made by a witch for a vampire. It is only meant to wake to the touch of the undead, but it seems the bond you share with the vampire is enough."

I stared at her. That couldn't be right. "What do you mean?"

Her dark eyes held too many secrets. "I mean exactly as I say. Your sword was made for a vampire. Curious, that your Potentate would have it in his possession."

I shook my head, tossing my loose, drying locks over my shoulder. "No, you're wrong. The sword woke for the Potentate too. He was the last one to wield it. But he is not a vampire's human servant. He has aged at a normal rate."

She shrugged. "I do not know the man, but he has lied to you in one way or another. Either he did not actually wield the sword, or he is something other than he seems. Considering he gave it to you with the expectancy for it to wake, he suspected what you are."

My mouth went dry. If the Potentate knew what the sword would do, and had suspected what I was, having the sword wake for me would have confirmed it.

And yet here I was, still alive and free.

"I would be careful around this man," Ryllae said.

I nodded, my gaze distant. "I'm always careful."

I fell silent with too many thoughts coursing through my mind to articulate. And I wasn't sure I wanted to. I had known the Potentate nearly my entire life. What was going on?

The sun disappeared over the ruins of the old keep, letting the darkness slowly seep in from the ground up. I gasped, feeling it the moment Asher woke.

Ryllae put a hand on my arm. "Are you well?"

I let my breath out slowly as the sensation faded. "I think I just felt Asher waking. He will be here soon." I turned wide eyes to her. "I don't know why I am feeling so much, it was never like this before. I've even felt his emotions, but it was just for a moment, then it went away."

She glanced me over, as if there was something *else* I couldn't see. "I am not well-versed in the bond between vampire and servant, and even less so when the servant is a hunter, but these bonds do tend to strengthen with proximity."

I licked my lips, considering her words. "Do you mean it will get worse?"

"If it comes and goes, I'd say it already has. He's probably protecting you from much of it."

My stomach clenched painfully. If the bond would keep growing . . . Would I eventually become like any other servant? Would I lose my free will and identity?

I would kill us both before that happened.

Ryllae patted my arm. "I do not think it the most of your worries at the present."

I leaned against the wall and went quiet. I wasn't sure if that was true. It would be more true to say it wasn't my *only* worry. If the Potentate knew what I was, why hadn't he confronted me? I remembered his watchful gaze as

Steifan and I departed Castle Helius. Why was he watching me? What was he waiting for?

The sword at my back, which had helped me many times, suddenly felt like a mighty weight.

I stood in silence as darkness took full hold of the night.

Just when I would have started to worry, I heard Steifan and Tholdri approaching, and could sense Asher with them.

The three men rounded the corner and came into view. Steifan and Tholdri both seemed to blend into the darkness, but Asher's white hair and pale skin stood out like the moon. I shivered as I watched him approach, wondering if he really was blocking the bond between us to spare me.

His eyes were only for me as he reached us. He lifted a hand as if to touch me, then let it fall. "You defeated the Nattmara," he said.

I mustered a glare for Steifan and Tholdri, then turned my attention back to Asher. "I see *someone* filled you in."

He continued on as if my hostility did not exist, "And you have a plan for bringing your investigation to a close?"

I glanced at Ryllae, not sure how much she would want me to tell him.

She nodded once, her eyes wary. "Yes, we have a plan."

I realized Ryllae wasn't just protective of her secret,

she was actually frightened of Asher. At least someone was. It made me like her even more.

Asher watched me as Steifan unwrapped a piece of waxed parchment, then provided an enormous pastry.

The smell of cinnamon and pumpkin made my mouth water. I took the pastry with a lifted brow.

He grinned. "I thought you deserved a treat."

My laughter seemed to dissipate some of the tension. We had survived the Nattmara, and we had all but solved the murders. And Steifan knew the true way to my heart.

"We should go," Ryllae said with a mischievous smile. "We do not want to keep the Montrants waiting."

I grinned. I was actually excited to see what Ryllae could do, and to see the utter terror on Lord and Lady Montrant's faces. Frightening a confession out of them was far better than just killing them. I wanted to see them utterly disgraced before they went to the executioner's block. Not to mention, they could provide the names of any others involved.

Asher had watched the entire exchange impassively.

I pursed my lips, considering, and figured why not? He might be useful. "Do you want to come?" I glanced to Ryllae. "If it's all right with you?"

She considered for a moment, then nodded.

Asher seemed genuinely surprised. "An invitation from *my lady*? My, I thought this day would never come."

I narrowed my eyes. "Don't push it." I looked past him to Steifan and Tholdri. "Are you both ready?"

Tholdri grinned. "We were born ready."

I rolled my eyes, then led the way out toward the street. Tholdri and Steifan would be going through the gates, while Ryllae and I would take back to the canals. I thought it best if Asher came with us and not the men. I might trust him more than I wanted, but I still didn't trust him not to eat my friends. What did that say about our relationship? What did it say that I actually thought of it as a relationship?

As usual, too many questions not enough answers. Best just to focus on bringing justice. After all, it's what I did best.

Chapter Eighteen

Ryllae, Asher, and I waited at the ladder leading up into the Montrant's cellar. I tried to keep my breathing quiet as Asher listened for sounds coming from above.

After a moment, his silver eyes turned down to me, glinting in the light of my new lantern. "There are four people in the house, none in the cellar. We should be safe to go up."

Ryllae huddled close to me, her eyes a bit wide.

I turned to her. Still in her blood-stained dress, she looked ready to frighten the Montrants on appearance alone. "Are you sure you can do this?"

She stood a little straighter. "They won't be able to break through my glamour. They won't see any of us." She looked at Asher again. "But I will not lead them to their deaths, only to justice."

I finally realized what she was worried about. "Asher won't eat them. He can control himself."

Surprisingly, I believed my words. Asher would not be consumed by simple bloodlust.

Ryllae considered for a moment, then nodded and started up the ladder. She reached the top, then tugged the handle. "It won't budge. I think it's locked. They must have found the note."

She climbed back down, then Asher climbed up. He tugged the handle until metal groaned and wood splintered. He descended, then gestured for Ryllae to try again.

I watched her go up, then she opened the hatch and crawled into the cellar. I hoped her glamour would be enough. Now that the Montrants had seen the note, they would be wary. But that's why we had Asher too. If Ryllae's glamour failed, he could try to bespell them long enough for us to escape.

Tossing my cloak behind my shoulders, I ascended the ladder one-handed, setting my lantern on the wood floor above so I could climb out. The Seeing Sword was silent, just as silent as Ryllae as she waited in the cellar.

Asher came up next while I looked around with my lantern. The cages were gone, as were the bloody rags and any other signs the cellar had contained captives. Our note had given them time to clear away the evidence, but it would also prepare their minds for what was to come.

Asher listened again, one ear tilted toward the rooms

above us. He nodded, signaling we were clear to venture up the stairs. Once we had the Montrants in our sights, Ryllae's glamour would take over. She would conceal us, and frighten the Montrants into confessing.

If things went wrong . . . Asher and I would be there to clean up the mess. The Montrants would be brought to justice one way or another. If things went right, however, Steifan and Tholdri would be waiting outside in full hunter garb, ready to escort the criminals to make their confession to the Archduke.

We went up the stairs and opened the door leading into the estate. We were in the kitchen. A cast iron pot burbled over hot coals in the hearth, and smoked trout was already arranged on a wooden platter on the nearby table, but the cook was nowhere to be seen. It seemed the Montrants appreciated a late supper, which was convenient. They would be easier to frighten if they were both there to witness the phantoms.

Asher gestured for us to step back into an alcove at the sound of footsteps. I didn't like it, but I knew Ryllae would prefer if I were the one with my back pushed up against Asher instead of her. My skin tingled at his near-ness, even though he'd gone as utterly still as only the dead can manage. If I didn't know any better, I'd say my nearness made him uncomfortable. But I really didn't know any better, I had no idea what he was thinking. I wondered if he was blocking me from his emotions, and what I might feel if he let down that wall.

I didn't have time to consider it further. The footsteps retreated, taking the scent of smoked trout with them.

Ryllae stepped out of the alcove ahead of us, then hurried out of the kitchen.

We followed her down a narrow hall and past the dining room, plastering our backs against the wall just as the female cook emerged and headed back toward the kitchen to fetch the soup. If she saw us, Ryllae should be able to conceal us, but I wasn't sure what would happen if she ran directly into us.

We waited as the cook returned to the dining room with two porcelain bowls of soup. She headed back toward the kitchen again, then veered off without going inside. A moment later we could hear her feet on the stairs.

I kept my back pressed against the wall. "She must be calling them to supper," I whispered. "Where should we hide?"

Ryllae leaned in close to my ear. "I will need a clear view of them."

Asher had gone around us into the dining room. There were doors on two sides, and large cabinets surrounding the massive table. The far wall was lined with curtains covering tall windows. He opened one door and peeked inside, then motioned us over to peer into a small linen closet.

"Lyssandra and I can hide in here," he said as we approached his back. "We don't need a clear view, only Ryllae."

Ryllae pulled back one of the tall curtains. "I'm small enough, I shouldn't make much of a bulge."

She was right, as soon as she was behind the curtain, I couldn't see her at all, and she could peek out once the Montrants were focused on their food. She wouldn't even need to use glamour as concealment.

"We can all hide in the curtains," I decided.

Footsteps coming down the stairs preceded murmured voices.

Asher grabbed my arm and shoved me into the closet, turning to close the door so that it was open just a crack.

I resisted the urge to push him out of the way. The voices were too close. A moment later, the Montrants and a third presence entered the room. Asher moved aside for me to peer out the crack so I could watch as a middle-aged male servant seated Lady Montrant. Her husband sat across the table from her. Neither seemed to sense anything amiss, both focused on the bowls of soup the servant moved before them. He poured their wine, then went to stand stiff-backed across the room from my and Asher's hiding place.

I felt Asher at my back, peering through the crack above me. I could sense his excitement. It wasn't often one saw glamour from a pure-blooded Sidhe.

It started with a green light swirling at the head of the table. Small enough that one could pass it off as a trick of the eye. The servant was the first to notice. He stared at it, blinking.

The light grew, swirling larger.

Lady Montrant seemed to notice it next, though her back was to us so I couldn't judge her reaction. "Bellamy," her voice was barely audible.

Finally, Bellamy Montrant noticed the light. It swirled larger until it formed a feminine figure. Charlotte's features became clear. For the first time, I saw her just as she would have looked in life. Then her features sagged, her eyes bulged.

Lady Montrant screamed.

I searched for the servant, I couldn't see him anywhere in the room. He must have ran while everyone was focused on Charlotte.

"A phantom!" Lady Montrant shrieked, standing so abruptly that her chair went skidding across the rug.

Bellamy stumbled to his feet, slowly backing away. He turned to run, but another specter blocked his way, this one looking just like Duke Auclair. Ryllae had done a spectacular job replicating his likeness for someone who had only spied him a few times from afar.

"You killed me, Bellamy," Duke Auclair's specter moaned, clutching his bleeding neck.

Bellamy staggered back. "W-what do you want?"

Lady Montrant had crawled under the table, cowering with her hands over her head.

"You killed me," the duke's specter said again.

"You killed me," Charlotte echoed.

A wet stain grew across Bellamy's velvet pants. "Phantoms! What do you want of me?" he rasped.

"Confess!" Charlotte ordered.

The lanterns in the room flickered as an unearthly wind kicked up, tinged with the scent of the grave.

The duke's face began to rot. "Confess," he hissed, "or I will drag you to the underworld here and now."

Bellamy fell to his knees.

His wife had collapsed under the table, sobbing. "We must confess, Bellamy! Charlotte was my friend!" She started muttering apologies.

I would have almost felt bad if I didn't know what they had done, but I had seen Charlotte's body. I had witnessed the duke's murder. How many victims had ended up enslaved to vampires, or dismembered in the Nattmara's lair?

The phantoms moved closer to Bellamy, trapping him as their bodies continued to rot. The smell of decaying flesh reached my nostrils.

"All right!" Bellamy shrieked. "We will confess, just leave us!"

"Now," the duke demanded. "You will go to the Archduke now. We will be watching you. If you fail, I will drag you into eternal torment." Blood flowed freely down his neck, soaking the rug at his feet.

Trembling, Bellamy reached a hand under the table toward his wife. "Come. Come now."

She gripped his hand and allowed him to guide her from underneath the table. Duchess and Duke Auclair watched them both with scornful eyes.

Huddled together, the Montrants scurried out of the

room. Steifan and Tholdri would be waiting outside to make sure they followed through.

My breath eased out of me. It was done.

"Do you believe they will actually confess?" Asher said behind me.

I nodded, still staring out the crack. The specters began to fade. "If they don't, we will haunt them until they do."

"Why not just kill them yourself?"

I turned to face him, only able to see a sliver of his face from the light shining through the doorway. "You mean like I would kill a vampire?"

He nodded.

"If I could send vampires to the executioner's block instead of killing them myself, I would."

He watched me for a long moment. "There is a part of you that enjoys the bloodshed, Lyssandra. Do not lie to yourself."

I stepped closer to him, which didn't take much effort in the small space. "Yes, I enjoy the thrill of battle, but if you think for a second that I enjoy taking lives, the only one lying to themselves is you."

I turned away from him and pushed the door open, then stepped into the dining room. The duke and duchess were gone, and there was no hint of blood on the rug.

Ryllae stepped out from behind the curtains. "Was that adequate?" she said with a smile.

I looked her up and down. She seemed so small and harmless. "It was utterly terrifying."

Asher exited the closet behind me. "We should return to the cellar. I still hear others in the house."

I imagined the servant and the cook would be hiding for the rest of the night, but he was right. I wanted to regroup with Steifan and Tholdri as soon as they were dismissed by the Archduke.

I led the way down the hall, back through the kitchen, and into the cellar. I avoided Asher's gaze all the while. For some reason, what he said had bothered me. He really thought I enjoyed executing vampires.

In truth, I rarely regretted the deaths when the vampires were attacking me, but the executions . . . cutting off someone's head while they begged for mercy tended to stick with you. I did it because it was the right thing to do. That didn't mean it was easy.

I didn't know how to explain that to him. I didn't know how to explain why I would kill a defenseless vampire without blinking, when I would go to such elaborate lengths to scare humans into a confession.

I couldn't explain it to him, and I couldn't explain it to myself. But what was done, was done. Justice would always be served, one way or another.

Chapter Nineteen

The Montrants confessed to everything. The other guards and nobles involved were arrested, and every inch of the canals were scoured for the bodies. Bastien and Vannier were never located, which stung, but I couldn't search forever for a child who might not be found.

Three days after the events in the Montrant's cellar, Steifan, Tholdri, and I visited Ryllae to say our goodbyes.

Within her small home she embraced me, pulling away with a knowing look. "You be careful, and remember all we discussed."

I stepped back to stand between Steifan and Tholdri, acknowledging her words with a nod. I hadn't told either of the men my suspicions about the Potentate. Such thinking could be dangerous, and I didn't want them involved.

"If you ever find yourself in the North," I said, "come pay us a visit."

Her mouth twisted. "I find that unlikely, but if you run across any of my people in your travels, I will come."

Unfortunately, that was just as unlikely as her coming to visit. "We better be off," I said. "We have a long ride ahead."

Ryllae's mouth twisted further. "A word alone, Lyssandra, if you would."

Before I could answer, Tholdri patted me on the shoulder. "We'll wait for you outside."

Steifan followed him out, leaving me alone with Ryllae. I found myself nervous of what she might have to say. I already knew I had to worry about the Potentate. I wasn't sure what else she could tell me.

She stepped closer, craning her neck to look up at me. "I think you should ask your vampire about your sword. I believe together you could discover the reason it was created, and why it has found its way to you."

I furrowed my brow. "The Potentate gave it to me. It didn't find its way to me."

Her smile bordered on condescending. "Dear child, such objects go where they please. The sword would never have made it to you if that was not its wish."

I glanced at my sword hilt over my shoulder, once again thinking it might be more of a burden than a boon. "Whenever I see Asher again, I will ask him."

"You speak so casually," she laughed, "as if you will not be seeing him quite soon."

I narrowed my eyes. "I haven't seen him since the night we haunted the Montrants. How can I say when I will see him again?"

She hugged me again, muttering against my shoulder, "You will be traveling through dangerous lands. I have little doubt that he'll be watching over you."

"I thought you didn't like him," I said as she pulled away.

She shrugged. "I don't like any vampires. They are bloodthirsty monsters, but that does not mean that I cannot see the truth. He will be watching you, and protecting you. Whether that is a good thing or a bad thing is yet to be seen."

I smirked. "Your advice is confusing, as always."

"I fear I have no clear advice on this matter, but you are a clever woman. You will figure it out. *All* of it. Now off with you, the morning wears on."

I found myself sad to leave her. It was nice having another woman around. Maybe when I got back to Castle Helius, Isolde and I could have some girl talk. But then again, maybe not.

LATER, AS WE EXITED THE CITY GATES, WE WERE approached by two familiar faces.

Bastien grinned when he saw us, and parted from Vannier to run toward us.

I slid down from my horse and met him halfway,

scooping him up in a hug. I twirled him once, then set his feet on the ground. "Where in the Light have you been?" I gasped.

Vannier approached as Steifan and Tholdri reached us with our horses. "My old friend found him hiding in the slums. Someone had tried to take him, so he thought it best to lay low." Vannier patted Bastien's sandy hair. "He's a smart lad."

Bastien grinned. "When my grandfather found me we thought it best to hide until you solved Duchess Auclair's murder. Then we heard about the duke." His smile fell.

I looked to Vannier. "Grandfather, eh?"

His wizened cheeks reddened. "When we heard of the duke's death, I thought I might as well tell him. We will both need to search for new employment."

"Well I'm glad to see you both alive," I said. "Truly."

"Not that this isn't touching," Tholdri said to my back, "but we need to get moving."

"We will let you go," Vannier replied. "We just wanted to offer you our thanks. We could have ended up just like the duke and duchess, or the countless victims lost in the canals. We heard the Archduke is still weeding traitors out of the guard."

I nodded. "The Montrants gave many names, it will take time to question them all and punish the guilty."

Vannier wrapped an arm around Bastien's shoulders. "We can only hope they all get the block. Now we'll let you be on your way. I'm sure you have other innocents to save."

I gave Bastien a pat on the head. "You stay out of trouble now." My throat tight, I climbed back up on my horse, then urged it forward, not looking back. I'd never been good with goodbyes.

Together, Tholdri, Steifan, and I rode through the gates.

"If I didn't know any better," Tholdri said as our horses ambled down the bridge away from the guards, "I'd say Lyssandra has a weakness for children." When I glared at him, he winked. "I've never seen you grin like that. And you almost cried when we left him."

"I was simply relieved he didn't get killed because of us."

"If you say so," Tholdri teased.

The rest of the day's ride was pleasant and without issue. It was good to be on the road again, though I had my fears about returning to Castle Helius. Beyond that, I had promised to help Asher figure out who had killed the other ancient. I wasn't entirely sure I was up to the task, and I wasn't even sure when he would find me again.

Yet that night, Ryllae's words held true. I sensed his presence in the darkness, watching over me. Part of me wanted to find him and chase him off. Yet another part, a small dark part I would never admit to, took comfort in knowing he was there.

Sneak Peek at Blade of Darkness

The night air in the mires was warm and balmy, scented heavily with grasses and muck. I waited with my back against an old abandoned cottage, the boards half-rotted and crumbling. It was unwise to be alone in the mires at night with only my horse, but I wouldn't be alone for long. An ancient vampire was coming to meet me. Any ghouls hoping to tear me limb from limb wouldn't stand a chance.

I looked up at the crescent moon, trying to guess what time of night it was. The letter had said midnight, of course. Asher, like many of the older vampires, had a flair for the dramatic.

The tiny hairs on my arms prickled as I sensed him out in the darkness, his presence like a second heartbeat thrumming in my head. I had hoped the week we had spent apart would lessen the bond between us, but I realized with sudden surety that it hadn't. Our growing bond would not so easily be undone.

"Hello, Lyssandra."

I turned toward the sound of his voice, peering around the corner of the dilapidated cottage. He stood framed in moonlight, his long white hair lifting in the wind.

I stepped out into the open. "It's about time."

"It is precisely midnight."

I rolled my eyes, then started walking toward him. I felt naked without my armor, but this was no official mission. No, I was going directly against my duties as a hunter of the Helius Order. "Sending a courier to Castle Helius wasn't exactly subtle of you."

I had moved near enough to see the corners of his pale lips curl upward. "Would you rather I had delivered the letter myself?"

I crossed my arms, bunching up my blue linen shirt. "You would be dead if you had."

He lifted one black-clad shoulder in a half shrug. "Perhaps." He glanced around. "I had expected you to bring Steifan and Tholdri."

I tossed my red braid behind my back as I shook my head. "No, I don't want them involved in this. It's too dangerous. Neither of them would stand a chance against something that could murder an ancient vampire."

"I'm glad to hear you think of it as *murder*." He stepped closer, invading my personal space. "You're free to begin tonight?"

I craned my neck to meet his silver eyes so near. "I can give you tonight and three nights after that, then I must return to Castle Helius."

He moved a little closer and I put a hand on his chest to stop him. The Seeing Sword at my back didn't utter a single warning. It really didn't see him as a threat. I supposed neither did I, not anymore. "What is with you tonight? You're usually not this pushy."

Seeming a little startled, he stepped back. "Forgive me, I had forgotten what the bond feels like when you're near."

"It's only been a week."

"Time moves both slowly and quickly when you've been alive as long as I have." He stepped further back and looked at my horse. "You will not need your mount for long. She'll have difficulty reaching Evral's lair."

I lifted my brows at the mention of the murdered vampire. "What, did he live up a tree?"

"Up a mountain. A steep, rocky mountain."

"Of course," I sighed. "He couldn't make things too easy."

"I'm sorry his death is such an inconvenience."

I gave him a poignant look. "That's not what I meant and you know it. Now we should get moving. I don't want to get stuck up on a mountain top when you have to flee the sun for the day."

"We won't reach the lair tonight," he explained. "But you are right, we should start moving. I know somewhere you can stay and stable your horse."

I glanced at my horse, feeling almost guilty for having taken her. She was bred and trained to carry hunters into battle. Not to carry traitors while they investigated vampire murders.

I hadn't heard Asher move, but suddenly he was standing close again. "Your thoughts play across your face. You feel guilty."

I sucked my teeth, irritated that he could read me so easily. "I take my oaths seriously, as you know, else I wouldn't be here."

"Have you figured out yet why the Potentate entrusted you with the Seeing Sword?"

"That's none of your concern." I stepped away, then started walking toward my horse, not wanting him to see my expression.

Because I hadn't learned anything. I hadn't learned why the Potentate would give me a sword that would only awaken for a vampire or a vampire's human servant. I hadn't learned why he sent me to Silgard, or why he never questioned Karpov's demise.

But I could admit, if only to myself, that my suspicions were part of why I was standing in the mires with Asher in the middle of the night. The Potentate had sent me away right before the ancient was murdered. Perhaps it was a coincidence, but I was beginning to learn that few things in life were actual coincidences. Not when powerful men shaped your fate. Not when ancient vampires stalked you from the shadows.

So here I was, prepared to solve a vampire murder,

and to stop the other ancients from being killed. To stop a *particular* ancient from being killed, because if someone was trying to overthrow the old order, he had a target on his back as much as any of us. His death would end me too. I didn't want to die, and maybe, just maybe, I didn't want him to die either.

Note from the Author

I hope you enjoyed the second installment of the Duskhunter Saga! Please take the time to leave a review, and visit my website to learn more about this and other series.

www.saracroethle.com

The Moonstone Chronicles

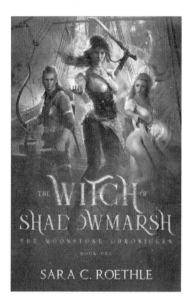

When the fate of the elves rests on the shoulders of an antisocial swamp witch, will a common enemy be enough to bring two disparate races together?

The Empire rules with an iron fist. The Valeroot elves have barely managed to survive, but at least they're not Arthali witches like Elmerah. Her people were exiled long ago. Just a child at the time, her only choice was to flee her homeland, or remain among those who'd betrayed their own kind. She was resigned to living out her solitary life in a swamp until pirates kidnap her and throw her in with their other captives, young women destined to be sold into slavery.

With the help of an elven priestess, Elmerah teaches the pirates what happens to men who cross Arthali witches, but she's too late to avoid docking near the Capital. While her only goal is to run far from the political intrigue taking place within, she finds herself pulled mercilessly into a plot to overthrow the Empire, and to save the elven races from meeting a bloody end.

Elmerah will learn of a dark magical threat, and will have to face the thing she fears most: the duplicitous older sister she left behind, far from their home in Shadowmarsh.

Tree of Ages

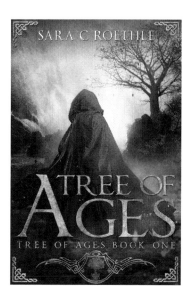

A tree's memory is long. Magic's memory is longer, and far more dangerous.

After a century spent as a tree, Finn awakens into a world she barely recognizes. Whispers of the Faie, long thought destroyed, are spreading across the countryside, bringing fears that they are returning to wreak havoc amongst the mortals once again.

Dark shapes lurk just out of sight, watching Finn's every move as she tries to regain the memories of her past. As if by fate, travelers are drawn to her side. Scholars, thieves, and Iseult, a sellsword who seems to know more about her than he's letting on.

When one of Finn's companions is taken by the Faie, she will be forced to make a choice: rescue a woman she barely knows, or leave with Iseult in search of an ancient relic that may hold the answers she so desperately seeks.

Her decision means more than she realizes, for with her return, an ancient evil has been released. In order to survive, Finn must rediscover the hidden magics she doesn't want. She must unearth her deepest roots to expose the phantoms of her past, and to face the ancient prophecy slowly tightening its noose around her neck.

The Will of Yggdrasil

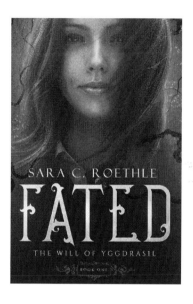

The first time Maddy accidentally killed someone, she passed it off as a freak accident. The second time, a coincidence. But when she's kidnapped and taken to an underground realm where corpses reanimate on their own, she can no longer ignore her dark gift.

The first person she recognizes in this horrifying realm is her old social worker from the foster system, Sophie, but something's not right. She hasn't aged a day. And Sophie's brother, Alaric, has fangs and moves with liquid feline grace.

A normal person would run screaming into the night, but there's something about Alaric that draws Maddy in. Together, they must search for an elusive magical charm, a remnant of the gods themselves. Maddy doesn't know if she can trust Alaric with her life, but with the entire fate of humanity hanging in the balance, she has no choice.

FATED is Norse Mythology meets Lost Girl and the Fever Series.

The Thief's Apprentice

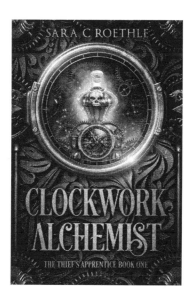

The clock ticks for London...

Liliana is trapped alone in the dark. Her father is dead, and London is very far away. If only she hadn't been locked up in her room, reading a book she wasn't allowed to read, she might have been able to stop her father's killer. Now he's lying dead in the next room, and there's nothing she can do to bring him back.

Arhyen is the self-declared finest thief in London. His mission was simple. Steal a journal from Fairfax Breckinridge, the greatest alchemist of the time. He hadn't expected to find

Fairfax himself, with a dagger in his back. Nor had he expected the alchemist's automaton daughter, who claims to have a soul.

Suddenly entrenched in a mystery too great to fully comprehend, Arhyen and Liliana must rely on the help of a wayward detective, and a mysterious masked man, to piece together the clues laid before them. Will they uncover the true source of Liliana's soul in time, or will London plunge into a dark age of nefarious technology, where only the scientific will survive?

Clockwork Alchemist is classified as Gaslamp Fantasy, with elements of magic within alchemy and science, based in Victorian England.

Xoe Meyers

I am demon, hear me roar.

Xoe has a problem. Scratch that, she has many problems. Her best friend Lucy is romantically involved with a psychotic werewolf, her father might be a demon, and the cute new guy in her life is a vampire.

When Xoe's father shows up in town to help her develop her magic, it's too little too late. She's already started unintentionally setting things on fire, and he lost her trust a long time ago.

Everything spirals out of control as Xoe is drawn deeper into the secrets of the paranormal community. Unfortunately, her sharp tongue and quick wit won't be enough to save Lucy's life, and Xoe will have to embrace her fiery powers to burn her enemies, before her whole world goes up in flames.

Twilight Hollow Cozy Mysteries

An inept witch, a cozy town, and an old dark magic.

Welcome to Twilight Hollow, WA, a small forest town with three resident witches. Adelaide O'Shea runs the Toasty Bean, imbuing her coffee and tea with warm, cozy magic. When a black cat crosses her path, she worries her new pet might be unlucky, and her suspicions are confirmed when the next thing in her path is a dead man with her phone number in his pocket.

And the cops aren't the only ones breathing down her neck over it. There's an old, dark magic in town, and it has its sights set on Addy. With the help of her two witch sisters, a handsome detective, and a charming veterinarian, can Addy solve the murder and escape the darkness? Or will she and her new spooky pet have to turn tail and run?